Renegade
Husband

To Anita Higman who always thrills me with her fresh perspective to life. Thank you for your friendship.

A note from the Author:
I love to hear from my readers! You may correspond with me by writing:

DiAnn Mills
Author Relations
PO Box 719
Uhrichsville, OH 44683

ISBN 1-59310-523-1

RENEGADE HUSBAND

Our mission is to publish and distribute inspirational products offering exceptional value and biblical encouragement to the masses.

All scripture quotations are taken from the King James Version of the Bible.

All of the characters and events in this book are fictitious. Any resemblance to actual persons, living or dead, or to actual events is purely coincidental.

PRINTED IN THE U.S.A.

Or check out our Web site at www.heartsongpresents.com

Caleb Windsor woke with a start. Sweat streamed down his face.

His heart pounded like a trapped rabbit, and his mind grappled with reality. He rubbed his face and attempted to focus in the utter blackness. The same nightmare plagued him again, the fifth time in the last month. He'd been accused of stealing horses, and someone had swung a rope over a tree limb and around his neck. That someone was his brother Christopher.

He moaned, not in physical pain but in spiritual anguish. Wanted posters throughout the territory publicized Caleb's picture as the "bad Windsor twin." The brothers shared identical looks but little else. Caleb was the oldest, and he'd always shouldered the blame for Chris's actions. Each time, Caleb hoped and prayed his younger brother would change. As of yet, no amount of repentance had caught Chris's attention. But Caleb hadn't given up, although the thought of swinging from the end of a rope left a mighty bitter taste in his mouth.

DIANN MILLS lives in Houston, Texas, with her husband Dean. They have four adult sons. She wrote from the time she could hold a pencil, but not seriously until God made it clear that she should write for Him. After three years of serious writing, her first book *Rehoboth* won favorite **Heartsong Presents** historical for 1998. Other publishing credits include magazine articles and short stories, devotionals, poetry, and internal writing for her church. She is an active church choir member, leads a ladies Bible study, and is a church librarian.

Books by DiAnn Mills

one

Spring 1885

"Mama, I want an adventure. Something real. And something more exciting than the Nebraska prairie." Audra Lenders stood in the doorway of their soddy and gazed out over the flat land to where the earth and sky met. A pretty sunrise in shades of pink and purple blended together until she could not tell where one color ended and another one began. Birds welcomed the day, their song a bit sweeter this morning. "There is so much of this world I want to see."

"Mercy, Audra. Have you been thinkin' about Pastor Windsor's son again?" Her mother's shrill voice pierced Audra's ears. She loved Mama, but when she became exasperated about something, her voice rose like a screech owl.

"A little. After all, I did tell him I'd think about it." Audra turned to study the worry lines around her mother's eyes as Mama labored over a list of supplies for her and Papa to purchase this morning.

Mama glanced up and shook her head. "You know Papa and I don't think it's a good idea for you to travel all the way to Colorado by yourself and then possibly be disappointed. Why, you don't even know this man. Look around you. Archerville has fine men who'd be honored to have you for a wife."

"None of the young men from Archerville interest me. I want a love like in the Bible. The men around here treat me fine, but I can't picture myself married to any of them."

"You're asking for the impossible. Take your mama's advice and stay where you are."

"If Pastor Windsor's son isn't right for me, I'll find a job and earn the money to come home." Audra crossed her arms

5

and returned her attention to the peacefulness outside.

"As stubborn as you are?" A lock of Mama's light brown hair with wisps of gray slipped from her bun onto her neck. She laid her pen aside to tuck back the stray lock. "I'm afraid you'd stay in Colorado rather than admit a mistake."

"My stubbornness is exactly why I wouldn't marry a man who wasn't fittin'."

Mama glanced up. "I do hope you'd return to a family who loves you." Her pale blue eyes softened. "But isn't where we live enough of an adventure?"

The hot grueling summers and the winters that delivered whirling snow and freezing temperatures were not Audra's idea of an exciting journey. The only home she'd known was this soddy—dark, damp, and smelly. Oh, for something different! "Remember when you were younger? Didn't you want to do something more than what everyone expected? See more of our country?"

Mama laughed. "That's why I left Kentucky and married your papa."

"See, you *do* understand."

"I loved your papa, and heading into new territory with my husband was quite different from boarding a train and stagecoach. You don't know a soul in Colorado. Strangers, all of them." She held up a finger. "Outlaws roam that territory—horrible, evil men who care about nothing or no one but themselves. I refuse to think about what might happen to you. How will I ever rest knowing you're there? What if Pastor Windsor's son is not kindhearted?"

"Mama, I already told you what I'd do if we didn't suit each other. Besides, all we're talking about are the 'ifs' and not a word about God's plan."

Her mother picked up the pen and dipped it into the ink well. "Are you reading His Word?"

"Of course I am. I want to be in God's will." By now, Audra felt an inkling of doubt, not with her desire to leave or the surety of God wanting her to go but with her parents giving permission. Perhaps they had decided the matter and no amount of talking would persuade them.

"You keep reading," Mama said. "Sometimes we overlook what God is saying, because we seek permission to do something rash."

Audra gasped. "I'd never do such a thing. Why, that's pure selfishness."

Mama tilted her head. "You could be in the middle of sin and not recognize it at all."

Audra bit back a remark. Her thoughts strayed far from respectful, but she understood her mother spoke out of love. Mama and Papa's reservations must stem from the fact that she was the youngest of their eight children.

Hours later while Mama and Papa were gone for supplies, Audra reflected on her mother's words. The thought of looking for a passage in the Bible to clear her way to Colorado unnerved her. She had searched the scriptures for an answer and felt confident of God's blessings. In the quiet of her spirit, she sensed her heavenly Father urging her to make the journey and to consider a role as Christopher Windsor's wife. Not one single passage had convinced her but rather several had spoken to her. All gave her strength and reassurance to trust God above all things. She'd read about Abraham and Sarah setting out for the promised land and understood not everything about Colorado would be perfect. She'd read about Isaac and Rebekah, and Jacob and Rachel—and attempted not to dwell on their problems. But Audra sensed the greatest blessing in reading about Ruth. *Whither thou goest, I will go: and where thou lodgest, I will lodge: thy people shall be my people, and thy God my God.*

Those words pressed against her heart. Surely this was Pastor Windsor's bidding—God's bidding—to become a pastor's wife. Christopher Windsor had to be a good man. How could he be any different from his father?

Audra busied herself in the warm sunshine and finished her chores. She relished the fact that winter was now behind them. She'd always treasured the first gentle snowfall but, as the months plodded along, she grew tired of the endless drifts and biting cold. Promises of spring put those dreary days aside and birthed new ideas for the future.

Her mind drifted back to Pastor Windsor's last visit.

"Audra, consider marrying Christopher. He's a fine man who loves the Lord. His church is growing, and he needs a wife, a pretty one like you to walk beside him." He reached inside his jacket and pulled out a photograph. "Twins." He grinned and handed her the photograph. Indeed they were identical. Pastor Windsor pointed to the young man on the left. "That's Christopher. The other one is Caleb, and he's a rancher."

The young men resembled their father. Thick hair, large eyes, and wide smiles drew her instantly into a dream world. They looked to have dark brown hair like the pastor, maybe his midnight blue eyes, too. Audra never met Mrs. Windsor; she'd died giving birth to the boys.

Having the pastor speak for his son wasn't the kind of proposal she'd always dreamed of. But the idea of it all challenged her. She wanted the opportunity to meet this Christopher Windsor and see if they could learn to love each other.

With a sigh, Audra strode toward the sod barn to gather eggs. Mama had taken several with her to trade for supplies in town, depleting the ones they had for their own use. Audra found a half dozen and took them into the house before heading for the garden. After pulling a few weeds from around sprouting vegetables, she picked up a pail. The thought of fresh, tender greens for tonight's dinner made her mouth water. Glancing about at the pastel-colored wildflowers shooting up from the spring earth and the sight of new calves and colts exploring the world, Audra had to admit she'd miss the prairie's spring beauty. This was all she'd ever known, but a yearning deep inside compelled her to move beyond the familiar boundaries to the western mountains. The idea of green valleys and aspen trees with an abundance of different kinds of animals and birds made her feel giddy. She'd never seen bighorn sheep or water roaring so fast it foamed up white.

"Give me your answer as soon as you can," Pastor Windsor had said during the last evening visit. They'd been sitting at the table after dinner. Papa enjoyed discussing the Bible, but the pastor obviously had other things on his mind. "I'd write Christopher and make all the arrangements for you. In his last letter, he said he was looking for the Lord to give him a wife."

"I can't go without Mama and Papa's blessing," she said.

Papa cleared his throat. "I promised myself that my daughter would never marry sight unseen. I want her to be happy."

"I understand, and I agree," the pastor said. "I'd make sure Christopher provided a place for Miss Audra to stay until they got to know each other."

"It's not what I envisioned for my Audra," Papa said.

"Then I'll be praying God reveals His plan to all of us."

O Lord, please let all of us be in agreement about this. And I do so want to go.

Audra's mind continued to replay Pastor Windsor's request. As late evening took on the colors of sunset, she fed the animals and milked the cow. On through preparing dinner, she wished she knew Mama and Papa's decision. Most girls her age were married and had families. At twenty, she saw her dreams of a good husband slipping through her fingers.

Long after dark, Audra heard the wagon creaking across the prairie. She'd been rocking on the front porch when the sun finally rested for the day. The insects serenaded her as the darkness brought on the quiet. She tugged at her shawl. The night had grown chilly. She believed her destiny lay in Colorado; now she prayed God gave her parents the same revelation.

"Are you waitin' dinner?" Papa said.

"Sure am. It's ready and still hot."

"What are we having?"

Audra laughed. Papa must be powerful hungry. "Smoked ham, fresh greens, cornbread, and a sweet berry cobbler with lots of cream—and fresh coffee."

"You're going to make some man a good wife."

With those words, he caught her attention. If not for the darkened shadows, she would have tried to read his thoughts by the look on his leathery face. Silence leaped between them. Not willing to let a light-hearted moment vanish, Audra scrambled for words. "Me? A wife? Papa, who would have me? I'd rather go hunting or fishing than stay indoors."

"Perhaps Christopher Windsor can tame your wild spirit."

Audra startled then trembled. Had she heard correctly? "Papa?" Her voice came out barely above a whisper. All she could see of him was his tall lean frame, not the dark hair and bushy eyebrows or the set of his jaw.

Not a word passed between them. She tore her attention to Mama, who appeared to be shivering in the evening breeze.

"What do you say we get these supplies unloaded so we can eat?" Papa made his way to the back of the wagon, and she followed alongside Mama. "While we're enjoying that fine cobbler, we have much to talk about."

Mama sniffed, and Audra knew for certain it had been decided. She'd go to Colorado.

❧

Six weeks later, a letter arrived from Earnest, Colorado, addressed to Mr. Samuel Lenders. While they sat around the fire before bed, Papa read the letter. Audra longed to hear the contents, but she knew Papa needed time to think on what Christopher Windsor had to say. Finally he folded the missive and placed it in his Bible.

"He has an older couple for you to stay with—a Jed and Naomi Masters. They're good folks and are looking forward to having you in their home. You can live with them for as long as you like. The parsonage needs a little repair, and he's already begun work on it."

Audra nodded and refused to look at Mama. The tears had flowed much too frequently during the past weeks. *A home of her own? A real home?*

"One more thing. He sent money for your travel and mine. He thought it only fittin' that I accompany you to Earnest.

We'll take the Union Pacific out of Omaha and ride it to Denver. From there we'll take a stagecoach south to Earnest. I do say he must fare well as a preacher to afford this luxury." He eased back in his chair and stared into the fire. Taking a puff from his pipe, he continued. "And. . .he thanks you for considering marriage and me for allowing this unusual courtship. He promises to love you proper like the Bible says."

This time Audra felt her eyes moisten. She quivered at the mere thought of the future. She felt certain of God's hand in this, and now Papa would make the journey with her. What more could she ask?

"I wish Colorado were closer." Mama dabbed her nose with a handkerchief. "The thought of never seeing my little girl again is hard, real hard."

Audra took Mama's hand. "You have all of your other children and grandchildren close by, and with the railroad we can visit."

"The trip would be costly, I'm sure."

Audra forced a smile. She hadn't anticipated the pangs of loss to cut her so. She wished the money was there for Mama to come, too. "I will make sure I have chickens for egg money, so I can come home."

Mama sighed. "Promise me."

"I promise."

Papa took the letter from his Bible and reread it. Audra wished she knew the many thoughts rolling around in his head; even more so, she wondered what Christopher had written. Papa was prone to a serious nature, and she understood her leaving grieved him.

"If something goes wrong out there," he said, "if this man is not what he seems and you don't want to stay there, I'll come after you. I have a bad feeling about this, but I can't seem to discern if it's a papa not wanting his daughter to leave or a warning from God."

A chill swept over Audra, and her stomach twisted. *This is what I'm supposed to do. This is God's purpose for my life.*

two

Caleb Windsor woke with a start. Sweat streamed down his face. His heart pounded like a trapped rabbit's, and his mind grappled with reality. He rubbed his face and attempted to focus in the utter blackness. The same nightmare plagued him again, the fifth time in the last month. He'd been accused of stealing horses, and someone had swung a rope over a tree limb and around his neck. That someone was his brother Christopher.

He moaned, not in physical pain but in spiritual anguish. Wanted posters throughout the territory publicized Caleb's picture as the "bad Windsor twin." The brothers shared identical looks but little else. Caleb had always shouldered the blame for Chris's actions. Each time Caleb hoped and prayed his younger brother would change. Each time he was disappointed. But Caleb hadn't given up, although the thought of swinging from the end of a rope left a mighty bitter taste in his mouth.

Folks compared them to Jacob and Esau—with Caleb as the wayward brother who rebelled against God and all their father had taught. He refused to deny the accusations, and each time he took the punishment. Now he wondered if all those years of covering up for Chris was wrong. He'd pleaded with his brother to stop the lawbreaking, but the last time they talked Chris merely laughed. The next Sunday, he preached on forgiveness and gave the example of his outlaw brother Caleb Windsor. Chris had to be stopped, but how?

Chris could resolve this very minute to start living right and stop hiding behind his title as pastor. Every robbery and cattle rustling report would end if he'd repent and mend his ways.

Caleb knew one of his worst mistakes came in convincing

his brother to take a wife. In the beginning he thought the idea might work. He'd always heard a good woman settled down the worst of characters. But now his conscience screamed at him. How stupid to bring an innocent woman into the heat of this ruse.

"Get married," Caleb had said. "Take a wife and settle down. Leave this life behind. Start a family, and stop thinking of ways you can steal from honest folk. I'll even head to Mexico, and you can start over. No one will ever know the truth."

Chris eyed him for several long moments. A wide grin spread over his face. "I think I will. A pastor needs a wife, makes him look good in the community."

Caleb wanted to land a fist up alongside his brother's jaw. "The purpose is to stop this thieving life of yours. I'm giving you a chance to be an honest man."

His brother laughed long and hard, and it further served to feed Caleb's frustration. "You forget. I am the honest man."

"You mean you'd use our father and a God-fearing young woman to continue what you're doing?"

Chris chuckled, the devious low laugh that had become a part of him since they were little boys.

"I'll find a way to stop you," Caleb said. "You never have enough. It's always one more job—a little more money or cattle or horses to drive south."

"Be careful. I haven't gotten this far by being stupid. I have everything worked out, and getting caught isn't part of the plan."

That was over three months ago.

Caleb rested his head in his hands and stared up at the starless night. How many nights had he slept in the open, on the run for crimes he hadn't committed?

At first he wondered why his brother requested a bride of his father's choosing rather than select one from Earnest, then he realized Chris's method made him look like a saint in the eyes of their father and the townspeople. Chris didn't care for anyone but himself. The woman due to arrive in less than a week didn't stand a chance for happiness, and who would listen to her complaints? No one in town had any knowledge of her—another part of his brother's scheme.

Caleb knew how cruel his brother could be; he'd lived with the treachery for twenty-five years. The only folks who knew the truth were Jed and Naomi Masters, but they were smart enough not to let on to Chris. The older couple kept Caleb informed of the goings-on. Good thing they did, or he'd have swung from a tree a long time ago.

Currently Caleb had two big worries to take before the Lord. One was his brother's rebellion, and the second stemmed from the young woman who was destined to be his brother's bride.

Lord, this is my fault, isn't it? I tried to play God in the name of love and then made things worse. My brother is masking his unlawful practices under the pretense of a pastor. I could be shot tomorrow for something I didn't do, and I have a feeling my brother would pull the trigger without a hint of remorse.

❧

Audra thought the railroad trip from Omaha to Denver had been somewhat of an adventure, except the less than palatable food in a few of the establishments along the way. She hid the churning in her stomach for fear Papa would insist they return home. When the train filled up with cigar smoke from a few inconsiderate passengers, she lowered the window. Within minutes, black soot covered her face and clothes. Papa didn't mind the coating of black dust. In fact, he claimed to enjoy every minute of the journey, and for that reason she said nothing about her personal distress. The train had continued *clickety clack, clickety clack*, as if eating every mile of the vast country.

Now she and Papa bounced along side by side on a stagecoach hitting bumps and holes until she felt certain every inch of her was black and blue. An older man seated across from them must not have bathed for six months, and his dirty and ragged clothes had seen better days. Greasy, gray strands of hair clung to his face and neck. Audra held her breath and exhaled out the side opening of the stage door when she sensed she'd surely faint away. Papa laughed and talked to the man as though he'd known him forever. But Papa always had time for folks; he wanted to make sure they knew the Lord. She did, too, but the saying that cleanliness was next to godliness seemed fitting in this case.

The wagon hit a bump just when she chose to take a gasp of air. The jolt lifted Audra straight up. Her head banged against the top of the door opening.

"Ouch." She pulled her head inside and reached up to touch the crown of her bonnet.

"Are you all right?" Papa asked. "Looks like you best keep your head inside."

"I'm fine, thank you." She rested her hand in her lap. "I'm enjoying the countryside, so different from Nebraska." Although she'd avoided the truth, Audra did appreciate the scenic beauty of Colorado. The mountains and rolling terrain along with thick, green grass and wildflowers filled her with anticipation of her new home—and probably a husband.

"We should be in Earnest in a few hours," the bathless gentleman said.

"Good." Papa shifted in his seat. "My daughter plans to make her home there."

The gentleman raised a bushy brow and nodded. "I'd say a gal as pretty as you will be married up real soon."

"She's picky," Papa said. "She won't be marrying the first man who comes courtin'."

Thank you, Papa.

"I've been lookin' for a wife—"

The moment the words left the man's mouth, the sound of rifle fire popped, followed by another. One of the drivers fired. Audra stiffened and grabbed Papa's arm.

"Don't you dare think of looking outside," Papa said just as the stage lunged ahead.

She didn't answer. Fright enveloped every inch of her. Her

gazed fixed on the man's greasy-looking beard. She held her breath.

"Best be sheltering your daughter from stray bullets."

Audra swung her attention to Papa's ashen face. If something happened to him, it would be all her fault for wanting to come to Colorado. His arm wrapped around her and pulled her head against his chest. "Pray," he whispered. "We need God's angels to carry us on to safety."

"God doesn't visit these parts much." The man's voice never wavered with the sound of desperate men's weapons exploding around them.

"Who are those men?" Papa asked.

"Outlaws. Most likely Caleb Windsor's bunch."

The name of Windsor seized Audra's attention, and Papa gripped her tighter. "I imagine it's not any kin to the preacher in Earnest," he said.

The man chuckled. Thank goodness, Audra found staring at Papa's right boot a little more pleasing than the man's beard. "Caleb is the preacher's twin brother."

Papa moaned. Audra's head throbbed. "The preacher's twin is an outlaw?" Papa asked. "I thought he was a rancher."

Why hadn't Christopher Windsor told her about this? Audra wanted to read Papa's gaze, but the commotion wouldn't permit it.

"Yeah. What a sad situation for brothers."

The stage slowed, and at first Audra believed the outlaws had given up, but when she got a glimpse of two men wearing bandannas riding alongside the stage, she realized the truth.

Audra couldn't stop trembling. All Mama's warnings about evil men flooded her mind.

"I won't let any of them hurt you," Papa said.

How could he stop them? He didn't carry a weapon.

The stagecoach stopped. "You folks climb out of there," a man said. "We don't aim to hurt you, just help ourselves to your belongings."

"Same thing," the bearded man said. "The law needs to put

this bunch out of their misery. String 'em up."

Neither Audra nor Papa replied. The door swung open, and a masked man grabbed Audra's arm.

"Keep your hands off my daughter." Papa spoke in a tone she'd never heard before.

"Shut up, old man, or I'll give you a taste of this." The masked man lifted his revolver and pointed it at Papa.

"Throw that gun aside, and I'll show you how a real man fights," Papa said in the same low tone she heard the moment before.

"Please." Audra gasped. "I'm coming." She refused to look at Papa and allowed the masked man to pull her from the stage.

"Take it easy on the girl," one of the outlaws, still on horseback, called. "All we want is their money and any gold jewelry or watches."

Another man threw her trunk from the top of the stage to the ground. She glanced at the drivers; one was slumped over the other. She didn't want to think about what had happened.

"What about the driver?" Papa asked. "Can I help him?"

"Too late," the other driver said. "He's gone."

Tears filled Audra's eyes, and Papa drew her to him. "It's going to be all right," he said. "Keep praying."

Breathing a simple request for help, Audra watched the outlaws search through her trunk. Her cheeks warmed as the men yanked out personal garments.

"I don't have anything in there for the likes of you," she said.

The outlaw who had requested she not be harmed glared down at her from his horse. "I'm sure you have money hidden in these clothes."

And indeed she did.

In short order, the precious money sewn in the hem of her dresses lay on the ground.

"You lied to me, little lady," the same outlaw said.

She lifted her head, but Papa tugged on her arm. "She was

trying to protect her money."

"I think she can speak well enough on her own," the man replied. He must have been the leader, for he nodded, and another outlaw searched Papa's pockets.

Audra studied the outlaw who had defended her—lean, muscular, and from under the brim of his dark brown hat she saw a splash of dark hair. He must be Caleb Windsor. And his identity must be why he asked that she be spared, or so she'd like to believe.

"Say something," The outlaw cocked his revolver.

She stiffened. "Yes, I lied, and yes, I'd do it again. So, are you Caleb Windsor?"

"You have a quarrel with that?"

"I only wanted to know who would stoop so low as to kill and rob innocent people."

The other outlaws laughed. Papa told her to hush.

"I bet you're the little lady sent to marry my brother." The man leaned against his saddle horn. He chuckled, and it made her even angrier. If not for the deceased driver and her fright, she'd have said more. "From the looks of your face and that yellow hair, my brother could have done a whole lot worse. Hope he can handle your sassy mouth."

A man of God wouldn't have need to hear my sassy mouth.

"Keep quiet, Audra," Papa said, or rather he growled at her like an angry dog.

"Is that your name?" Caleb Windsor's pewter-colored stallion reared as though the sound of his rider's voice startled him.

"Yes."

Caleb Windsor dismounted and walked toward her. Audra's heart thumped so hard she feared it would burst through her chest.

"Leave her alone." The moment Papa's words left his mouth, Caleb swung his fist into his cheek and sent him sprawling in the dirt.

Audra sank to the ground beside Papa. Blood oozed from the corner of his mouth. She said nothing for fear she'd be next. A gloved hand forced her to her feet. Caleb Windsor stared down at her. Amusement sparkled from his deep blue eyes. Contempt best described her reaction, and she did her best to tell him of his wretched nature through her gaze.

"I'm that bad, huh?" he asked.

"I wouldn't know, sir." His nearness frightened her beyond belief. She'd never forget the coldness in his eyes. And she could never forgive him for hitting her father.

"So it's sir now?" He peered closer into her face. "I think I shall steal a kiss from my brother's betrothed."

Audra took a step back, but he grasped her chin, lifted the lower part of his bandanna, and kissed her hard—too hard.

"Tell that to my preacher brother. I kissed his lady before he set eyes on her." He laughed. For a moment she considered the immense pleasure of spitting in his face, but her actions would place her on his level of wickedness.

"God have mercy on you," she said. "How horrible for a godly man like Christopher to have to claim you as a brother. If your poor father only knew what you've become."

"If you only knew." He touched the brooch on the left side of her traveling dress. She cringed, feeling certain his fingers upon the jewelry somehow soiled her. "I think I need this, Miss Audra. It will serve as a lovely memento of our brief time together."

"It belonged to my grandmother."

"Wonderful. Then we'll keep it in the family." He laughed. "Kindly remove it, or I will do it myself."

Audra's fingers shook as she clumsily unclasped the heirloom. Sticking her finger, she winced.

"What a pity." He wiped the blood from her finger with a clean handkerchief. She caught the initials of CWW embroidered on the corner and wondered why a man of such ill repute managed to carry a clean handkerchief. She could have used it to tend to Papa. Caleb stuffed it inside his pocket. "Good job." He turned to the foul-smelling man who had ridden in the stage with them. "Your warning helped us avoid a trap. Grab your horse, and let's get out of here."

Audra glared at the disgusting pair before her. One simply smelled of his evil deeds, the other reeked of treachery to the brother and father who served God and His people.

"We will meet again." Caleb mounted his horse and tucked the brooch into his shirt pocket. Cocking his revolver, he faced the driver. "Stay here for thirty minutes before you pull out. Understand?"

The driver mumbled a yes. Six men disappeared across what Audra had once believed was a beautiful land. Bending to aid Papa, she wished she'd never heard of the Windsor twins.

three

Audra viewed the storefronts of Earnest with a mixture of disdain and regret. Nothing of the original adventure met her expectations. The beauty of snow-capped mountains, the lush green countryside, and the gurgling ripple of water now held little attraction. She'd seen a dead man—his chest covered in blood—and she hoped the gruesome sight never crossed her path again. The deceased had a family and friends who loved and cared for him. It all seemed so senseless—the murder, the robbery, the insults thrown by Caleb Windsor and his gang. Combined with Papa's swollen face, her money stolen, Grandmother's brooch gone, and the whole nightmarish experience, she wanted to turn around and head back to Nebraska.

"Come back with me," Papa said. "I don't think you really want to be a part of this. How can I ever tell your mama that you are in a wonderful place? How can I leave you behind to fend for yourself?"

Audra chose to reflect on his words rather than reply. He spoke the truth. She wanted a godly family, not one overcome with strife. How could God want her to have a brother-in-law who was a thief and murderer?

"We don't have any money to go home," she said.

"I have two hands and a strong back."

Leaning her head on his shoulder, she could only sob. "Oh, Papa, I never meant to cause you such trouble."

He kissed her forehead. "None of this is your fault. Don't punish yourself by believing otherwise." He paused. "Look at all this beauty. It reminds me of a piece of heaven, but Satan has a hold here. We just saw his powerful grip. Better to live in a desert with God than in a palace with evil."

21

"Maybe we haven't met the good folks yet, the ones who love God." Audra wondered who she was trying to convince.

"I'm waitin'." His voice rang with bitterness. "I'm telling you the gospel truth. I'm not heading back to Nebraska without you or facing your mother with the truth of this uncivilized territory. From what I've seen so far, life here is godless."

At the moment, she agreed with his conviction. She needed only a precious few words to convince her to leave Earnest far behind. But another part of her wanted to give the town a chance.

The stage rolled to a halt and stopped outside the sheriff's office. Already a few men gathered around them, and she felt the whole ordeal was about to be put on display.

"Sheriff, I have a dead man," the driver said. "Caleb Windsor's gang jumped us."

From the stage window, she saw two men from the crowd lift the deceased man's body to the ground.

"Get him to the undertaker and someone fetch Belle and the girls," the sheriff said.

Audra closed her eyes. *Lord, help this poor family with their loss.*

"I have two passengers inside," the driver continued. "Might want to fetch the preacher, too."

"Someone else killed?" the sheriff asked.

"No, Sheriff, a young woman and her father are here on business to see him."

Papa opened the door and stepped down before assisting Audra from the stage. Her shaky legs nearly gave way. The sheriff stepped from the crowd and tipped his hat. "Afternoon, ma'am, sir, I'm Lee Reynolds, the sheriff here in Earnest." He had a mustache that grew from ear to ear.

Papa sized him up quickly. "We could have used you a few miles back."

"Looks that way. I'm real sorry about the holdup. I'll get the doc to take a look at you."

"I'm all right." He stuck out his hand. "Samuel Lenders,

and this is my daughter Audra. It would suit us best if we could see Pastor Christopher Windsor."

The sheriff moistened his lips. No doubt he sensed Papa's disapproval of the local law. Audra shared the same sentiments. "I'd take you myself, but I need to get a report from the other driver and tend to the dead man's widow."

"Shouldn't you be sending out a posse?" Papa asked.

Silence split the air so loudly that Audra could hear it crackle.

"What do you do for a livin'?" Sheriff Reynolds asked.

"Farmin'."

"You stick to farming, and I'll stick to upholding the law."

She held her breath. Papa had been riled enough for one day.

"Sheriff Reynolds," a man called.

Audra swung her attention in the direction of the voice, one that sounded vaguely familiar.

"Pastor Windsor." The sheriff grinned widely, or maybe it was his mustache. "These folks are here to see you."

Identical to his picture, dark-haired Christopher Windsor threaded his way through the crowd. He captured Audra's gaze and held it. Compassion was etched on his face. "Mr. Lenders, Miss Lenders, I just heard what happened. Please accept my apologies." He reached for Papa's hand then turned to her. "This is not at all how I planned our first meeting."

"And it's not what I wanted for my daughter—ever."

Mr. Windsor took in a deep breath. "I should have told you about my brother, but I wanted to spare our father."

"I am a man of my word, Pastor Windsor," Papa said. "The way I look at it, you deceived me and my family, and now you want my daughter to consider a life under these circumstances? I wonder where God is in all of this."

Audra had never seen Papa this red-faced.

Mr. Windsor smiled as though Papa's drilling was as commonplace as directions to the church. "Let's fetch your trunk and settle you in at the hotel. After you've rested and gotten something to eat"—he paused and studied Papa's face—"and cleaned up those cuts, we'll talk about the problems with my brother."

"I'd rather know when the next stage heads back to Denver."

Papa hadn't mentioned the lack of money; anger had a way of talking for a person. At least Mama claimed so.

Mr. Windsor stiffened. "I understand how you feel, but if you'll allow me to explain, I'm sure you'll feel differently."

Audra placed her hand on Papa's arm. "Can't we listen to him? We *have* come all this way."

Papa scowled. The purplish bruise on the side of his face obviously directed his temperament. She remembered a bad tooth on the same side of his face. No doubt it now hurt as well. "It's gonna take a lot of persuading to make me see things different."

Mr. Windsor sought out a young boy to carry the trunk to the boardinghouse. As they moved down the street, Audra glanced at the buildings: the barber and undertaker, general store, sheriff's office, telegraph, doctor's office, and a hotel advertising baths and meals. Farther down, she saw a white church and a small house. She guessed a blacksmith and livery were there somewhere, too. Most towns had them.

Inside the hotel, Papa stopped. "We can't do this. Those thieves took our money."

"Stay with me," Mr. Windsor said to Papa, "and I'll take Miss Lenders to the ranch that I spoke about in my letter."

"How far out of town is it?"

"A few miles. Shouldn't take more than an hour."

Papa glanced at Audra. Every bone in her body cried out for rest, but he had to hurt even more. "Could we drink a cup of water first?" she asked.

"I'll do even better." Mr. Windsor's every word soothed her trampled spirit. He may look like his brother, but he had the tone of an angel. "I'll buy us all a good meal, then we can take a wagon to Jed and Naomi Masterses' ranch where I made arrangements for Miss Lenders."

Papa didn't refuse. He eased into a chair in the hotel's restaurant, obviously feeling every bit of the journey and the blow to his face. Mr. Windsor requested soap and water for them, which cleansed Papa's battle-scarred face and lip. Lines deepened in his face. Audra nearly wept. The events of the day had shattered her dreams—the robbery, the killing, and Papa's beating. When the hotel owner offered a room free of charge, Papa declined. He wouldn't owe any man.

"Pastor Windsor offered a place for me to sleep, and those lodgings suit me just fine."

Once they ate, Mr. Windsor paid the bill and left them to secure his wagon and horse. Papa leaned against the straight-backed chair and dozed. She hated this for him, absolutely hated it. A short while later, Mr. Windsor returned with a short stocky man who looked to be about the same age as Papa.

"Mr. Lenders, Miss Lenders, this is Jed Masters. He drove into town to see if he could be of service." Mr. Windsor clasped the older man's shoulder. "He's been like a father to me."

Jed reached out and shook Papa's hand. "Afternoon, folks. I thought I'd help out the pastor, since tonight's Wednesday and he has services. I can take your daughter to the ranch. You, too, if you're needin' a place to stay."

Papa startled. Audra hadn't thought about Wednesday prayer meeting either.

"I'd wanted to see your place," Papa began, "but I can't ask the pastor to take us out there and return before evening." He glanced up at Mr. Windsor. "Can we visit the Masterses' tomorrow?"

"By all means."

Papa stood. "I'd like to take a few things from the trunk, if you don't mind." He lifted Audra's chin. "Does this suit you, daughter?"

"Yes, Papa, what you need is rest, and we can talk tomorrow."

"May I have a word with Miss Lenders before you leave?" Mr. Windsor asked.

Pleased with his request, Audra saw her father nod. The

younger man gestured toward the door. "While your father is gathering what he needs, I'd like to show you the church."

Although she felt every mile of the journey, the thought of seeing Christopher Windsor's church thrilled her. They walked the short distance to the freshly painted building. Wrapping her shawl about her shoulders, she glanced up at the steeple and the bell intended to call everyone to worship.

"I wanted you to see God's house." He opened the door. "The members are increasing each Sunday. More importantly, we have many fine people turning their lives over to the Lord."

"What a blessing." The dwelling reminded her of Pastor Windsor's church at home, and she told him so.

"Thank you." His midnight blue eyes radiated warmth, so different from the same-colored eyes that had stared at her earlier. "I'm glad you came, so very glad. May I call you Audra? I'd be honored if you would call me Christopher."

"Yes, of course."

"I feel I must apologize to you again about my brother's actions. He is an impetuous, wicked man, but I know God loves him as I do. I've tried everything to convert him to the ways of our Lord, but he refuses. After today, the wanted posters will add even more crimes."

"How very sad for you." Audra's heart ached for the man before her. She could only imagine the burden he carried for his outlaw brother. "I don't blame you for today, but like Papa, I wish I'd known the circumstances. We could have been prepared, although the warning would not have readied me for the bloodshed today. Do you know the family of the deceased well?"

"Yes, I do. I cannot rest my head tonight until I have ministered to Belle and her two daughters."

"I, too, feel an obligation to offer my sympathy."

"You are truly a rarity." Tears welled up in his eyes. "Father spoke so highly of you, and the thought of a lovely Christian woman to help me in my ministry caused me to omit the truth. I praise Him that you were not hurt. The thought of my brother striking your father grieves me." He paused. "I am so sorry."

Audra believed every word he spoke. She longed to touch his handsome face. Right then, she knew she could not leave Earnest until she grew to know this humble man.

ॐ

Caleb paced the kitchen of Jed and Naomi Masters. He had a bad feeling about today and the young lady due in to Earnest. The last time he talked to his brother, Chris had not changed his mind.

"I'm going to push for marriage as soon as she arrives," Chris had said.

"Why? You might not like her?" Caleb asked.

"Doesn't matter. Father said she was pretty and a good lady. Those two things are all I need to know."

"Are you going to put an end to your gang?"

Chris grinned. "Haven't decided yet. Maybe I should pray about it."

Caleb clenched his fists. "That's blasphemy. How can you mock God?"

"He knows I'm going to quit someday. Look at all I do for Him now."

At the sound of a wagon approaching, Caleb's thoughts reverted to the present. He watched Naomi lift the checkered curtain to see if her husband had made it back from Earnest.

"Jed's home," she said. "Maybe he has word about the young lady. Oh my, a young lady is with him." Naomi held her breath then patted the bun resting at her nape. "Caleb, hide in our bedroom until it's safe for you to leave."

four

Audra instantly liked Naomi and Jed Masters. They looked to be her parents' age and possessed some of their manner-isms. Both were rather short and round—which meant more to love. Naomi's supper tasted better than her own mother's cooking, although Mama didn't have the different foods that were available at the Masterses' ranch. As soon as Naomi opened her arms to her, Audra felt at home. Oddly, when she first met Mr. Masters, he didn't seem nearly as warm and hospitable, as though he were preoccupied. Perhaps he knew the deceased man.

As she lay in her bed at the ranch and glanced about the shadows, she fought exhaustion to pray one more time for the deceased man's family and all those involved in today's events. She wondered if she should return home with Papa or give Christopher an opportunity to court her. The handsome pas-tor did need a wife and, from his kindly ways, she determined he'd be a fine husband. The man had taken her breath away. Papa, on the other hand, regretted ever leaving Nebraska, and it would take some strong persuasion for him to think other-wise. Not that she blamed him. Confusion had hammered a wedge between honoring Papa and following what she'd believed was God's will.

With a heavy sigh, she allowed a tear to trickle down her cheek. Then another. The waterfall of anguish washed over her, releasing all the torment and pain of the robbery. Realizing Papa could have been killed, too, caused her to rise from the bed and secure her handkerchief. The moment she held the dainty cloth to her nose, she remembered Caleb wip-ing the blood from her pricked finger. What a detestable man. She hated him. Those feelings were wrong, and she knew it, but their vehemence assaulted her nevertheless. What kind of life could she have with Christopher when his brother was a murderer and thief? How would they explain a wayward uncle to their children? For that matter, how did the community view the pastor's integrity?

A light rap at the door grasped her attention.

"Audra," Naomi said. "I hear you crying. May I come in?"

Taking a deep breath, Audra opened the door. The moment she saw the tenderness in the older woman's face, she fell into her arms and sobbed. "I'm scared, and I don't know what to do."

Naomi patted her back as though she were a child. "What is God telling you, dear?"

"I don't know. I was so certain at home, but after today I can't think clearly."

In the darkness, Naomi held her tightly, urging Audra to cry out her sorrow and grief. "Some things are not what they always seem," she said.

Audra swallowed and attempted to speak without sobbing. "I know. I thought this land had to be the most beautiful place in the country. Now it's stained with blood."

"You saw things at their worst. Believe me. I know better days are coming."

"You mean when Caleb Windsor and his men are stopped?"

"I mean ending the violence and getting to the truth of the crimes here."

"Do you think it will happen soon?" Audra's heart pounded a little harder. Oh, how she wanted today sealed away in a forgotten memory.

"I think so. In fact, I suggest you mention to Pastor Windsor that you want the violence to end before you marry."

Naomi's words made perfect sense. "Papa might agree for me to stay with those stipulations."

"I understand from Jed that your papa will stay here until he earns the traveling money to go home."

She nodded and dabbed at her nose. "Poor Mama. She will be terribly upset."

"Let's pray about all this," Naomi said. And they did.

※

Caleb and Jed stole through the shadows to a grove of oaks behind the corral, avoiding any of the ranch hands roaming about. The reality of Jed's concealing their friendship and sneaking about his own land always hit Caleb hard.

"Miss Audra is pretty shook up," Jed said. "Christopher did a fine job of making sure you're now wanted for murder. I'm sorry. You didn't need me to remind you of how this situation keeps getting worse." The older man lifted his hat to scratch his baldhead. "I don't understand your brother at all."

"Who would ever believe you and I branded cattle all day?" Caleb stopped himself from saying things he had no right to say. Chris was his brother. "I don't understand his reason for robbing the stage that he knew Miss Audra and her father rode. And punching Mr. Lenders's face. It's as though he wants Miss Audra to change her mind about staying."

"I don't think she has much to do with it at all. The way I look at it, Chris wants you out of the territory. You've protected him for so long that he's gotten real confident. But he's also clever. He believes you'd never try to expose him."

"He's wrong there. Today convinced me he has to be stopped. Unfortunately, I could get myself strung up before it happens."

"Still having those dreams?"

"Yeah. What I once believed were purely nightmares now I think is God telling me to do something." Caleb saw the outline of his horse by the light of a three-quarter moon. "Brother against brother. Reminds me of the Civil War. At least then both sides believed they were right. This mess is different. Chris can't possibly justify what he's doing."

"You're right, son. Something has to be done soon, and I'm ready to help in any way I can."

"You always have. To make matters worse, my stupidity has Audra Lenders involved. She tried to sound brave this evenin', but I heard the fear in her voice."

"Did you see her?"

"Once. A very pretty young woman. No wonder Father convinced her to travel west. Maybe she'll head back to Nebraska with her father."

Jed reached for the bridle. "You wouldn't say that if you saw the fuss your brother made over Miss Audra and her father. Mark my word, Samuel Lenders will return to Nebraska without his daughter."

Caleb left the Masterses' ranch and rode into the hills—where he'd lived like a criminal for the past year. He knew the way with his eyes closed. The days of sleeping in his own bed on his sprawling ranch had vanished with the accusation of the first robbery. Fortunately Caleb had a good foreman who ran things in his absence—the only other person besides Jed and Naomi who knew the truth.

He'd prayed for God to show him how to stop his brother. Not a pleasant thought at all, but today a man had given his life for Chris's greed. This made one more time Caleb regretted all the years of protecting his selfish brother. The image of Audra Lenders stepping down from the wagon danced across his mind. She reminded him of an angel. The sun color of her hair gave her the innocent look of a child. Yet he sensed she had inner reserves of strength, judging by the little he'd heard while hiding in Jed and Naomi's bedroom.

Caleb stiffened in the saddle. He refused to allow Audra Lenders to marry his brother. The idea of one more innocent victim falling prey to Chris's selfishness caused a surge of anger to swell in him. Naomi might have to take charge of telling her the truth.

❧

Audra hadn't intended to sleep the morning away but, by the time she opened her eyes, the sun had nearly reached its peak. She stretched and noted sore muscles. Those things promised to fade, but not the anguish from yesterday. The memories would always tear at her heart.

After dressing, she stepped into the kitchen where the

smell of fresh coffee and breakfast filled the room. Naomi kneaded bread on the table. "There's bacon and biscuits left from this morning," she said.

"Thank you." Audra smiled. "I planned to rise earlier and help you."

"Nonsense, you needed your rest. How are you this morning?" Flour clothed Naomi's hands, and when she reached to scratch her nose, white dusted her face.

Audra picked up a towel and wiped off the flour from her new friend. "I'll be fine. I appreciate last night more than words can say."

"Glad I could help. Have you decided what to do?"

"Despite yesterday, I still feel like I'm supposed to stay. Papa, on the other hand, will want me to hurry home, and that is tempting."

Naomi gestured toward the stove. "Help yourself to the coffee. Your papa loves you and wants to make sure you're safe."

"I know."

"Jed said Pastor Windsor is bringing your papa today?"

"Yes, ma'am. I'm anxious to see if Papa is all right."

"A good night's sleep always helps." Naomi smiled. "How does a hot bath sound to you?"

"I'd love it." She poured a steaming cup of coffee. "I feel like I have dirt on me all the way from Nebraska."

The bath did wonders for Audra's sore body. The hot water even soothed her weary emotions. She nearly fell asleep again. Her mind repeatedly swept back to her encounter with Caleb. She shivered then focused her attention on his wonderful brother. The sound of Audra Windsor—Mrs. Christopher Windsor—rolled easily off her tongue. She imagined herself making calls with Christopher, playing the piano on Sunday morning, listening to him prepare his sermon. . . Her dream world lingered like a fantasy.

Finally she forced herself from the metal tub, which strongly resembled a watering trough for animals. No sooner had she dressed than she heard dogs barking. From the bedroom window she saw Christopher and Papa seated atop a buck-board. Audra scrambled to pin up her hair, pinch her cheeks, and smooth the skirt of her favorite light blue dress with little pearl buttons lining the bodice. Taking a deep breath, she hurried from the bedroom.

Papa looked so much better. His face no longer held the drawn pallor from yesterday. He actually smiled when he saw her rushing to him.

"You look well, Audra," he said with a quick hug.

"And so do you."

He chuckled. "I fell asleep before the sun went down and woke this morning like a new man. Unfortunately, I missed last night's church services, but the pastor and I have had a fine talk this day."

"I'm glad to hear that." She wondered if he'd changed his mind. A part of her wanted all the things Colorado had to offer. Another part wanted Papa to protect her from the world. But Audra knew her girlhood days were over, and she needed to step out in faith for whatever God planned.

"As soon as I bid Mr. and Mrs. Masters a good day, I'd like to talk." Papa wrapped his arm around her waist. "I believe we have a fine man here," he whispered.

She glanced at Christopher, who captivated her with a boyish smile. She quivered at his gaze. What more could she possibly ever want?

A short while later, Audra and Papa strolled across a green pasture. In the distance several horses fed on fresh grass while colts played tag between their mothers. The sun shone warm and pleasant. She found it easy to forget the ugliness of the day before.

"I believe Christopher Windsor will take good care of you," Papa said. "We've been talking since breakfast, and I like him. He can't do a thing about his wayward brother but hope he realizes his failings." Papa shielded his eyes from the sunlight and paused. "Jed and Naomi Masters are good people, too. So I'm leaving you in their capable hands with my blessings."

Audra flung her arms around his neck. "Thank you, Papa. I won't disappoint you, I promise."

"Daughter, you have never failed to satisfy me with your spirit for adventure. I hope things work out for you and Christopher, but remember you can always come home."

A veil of disillusion crept over her. She had her future, but Papa must now work to earn the money for his return home. If only she could help him. "I want to find work to help pay your way back to Mama."

Papa shook his head. "I won't hear of it. Christopher is loaning me the money, and I plan to sell off some cattle when I get home and repay him."

Audra gasped. However did Christopher manage to convince Papa to borrow money? "Are you sure?"

"God's been good to us, and your mama and I can do this. Besides, the law is after Caleb, and our money could be found any day."

"When will you have to leave?"

"Two days hence."

She blinked back the tears. Love for Papa and Mama overwhelmed her. She would finally be on her own. All that had happened must be the hand of God.

Naomi and Audra worked together cooking dinner, a roast with green onions and potatoes from the previous harvest. Beans simmered on a wood cook stove that Mama would have loved. The blend of smells filled the ranch house with a tantalizing aroma. Bread rose to perfection and baked until golden brown. While Audra stirred together a milk cake, Naomi took fresh lettuce and wilted it with bits of bacon and fat.

Christopher, Papa, and Jed stayed gone while Naomi and Audra busied themselves with supper. What could those men be doing? A twinge of jealousy nipped at her heart. She thought better of it and dwelled on the days ahead.

Supper could not have been more perfect than if the Lord Himself had eaten with them. The food, the conversation, and the laughter made for a glorious evening. Christopher even asked Jed to bless the food and their time together. She discovered Christopher had a sense of humor—a clever wit about him that could take the smallest thing and create laughter. She liked the quality; she liked it a lot. He looked fine tonight, dressed in blue jeans and a light blue chambray shirt. His eyes fairly danced when he looked at her, and she caught him gazing at her more than once. Her cheeks reddened, but the warmth of the attention left her tingly.

Once Naomi and Audra washed the dishes and put everything back in order, Christopher asked if she'd join him for a walk.

"Your father and I need to get started back to Earnest soon, and I'd welcome your company."

Audra untied her apron. Unfathomable glee filled her from head to toe. She hoped her enthusiasm didn't show. The last thing she wanted was Christopher to view her as a flighty schoolgirl. "I'm ready," she said, and he took her arm.

Outside, the moon shed faint light, but a myriad stars lit the way before them. And to think this honorable, godly man wanted to share this beauty with her.

"You are a beautiful young woman, Audra. I noticed right off that the blue in your eyes matches your dress. I will be the envy of every single man in the territory."

Grateful for the night to mask her blush, she rummaged through her mind for the proper words. "I don't know what I've done to warrant such compliments, Christopher, but you are more than welcome."

He laughed lightly. "Your father is a fine man. We had a good day together."

"He said the same about you."

"Then he shared his approval of our courtship?"

She toyed with a pearl button on her dress. She detested feeling this nervous. "Why, yes, he did."

"Wonderful. I think you and I feel a mutual attraction. Don't you agree?"

Dare she speak the truth or play coy?

"Oh, Audra, don't tell me I've seen something in your eyes that isn't so."

The hurt tone in his voice moved her. "You saw correctly. I'm sorry. I simply didn't know how to respond."

"Then shall we marry right away?"

Startled, Audra ceased her stride alongside him. "I thought we were going to get to know each other first."

"Of course we will." He shrugged. "Forgive me. I'm simply anxious."

"And I, as well, but I do want to spend a little time getting to know you before we pledge ourselves for a lifetime."

Christopher gathered her hands into his. "So you are going to leave this poor heart aching each time we are together? How can I enjoy your company when I know we will soon part?"

She couldn't help but smile at the dear man before her. She wanted to memorize his features, remember his words. "I promised Papa I wouldn't rush into marriage. I do hope you understand."

"Ah, I want to please him, too."

Audra recalled her conversation with Naomi the night before. "What I really wish is for your brother to be captured so we would never have to worry ourselves over him."

Christopher said nothing. "I pledge to you, sweet Audra, that I will use all the blessings of God to have Caleb brought into custody." He squeezed her hands lightly. "Now, if the sheriff captures him tomorrow, I will push you to name a wedding day. The members of my congregation will be so very happy." He pulled her to him and leaned his head toward her.

Audra's pulse quickened. She wanted Christopher to kiss her, but it was too soon. She took a step back, but he tightened the grip on her hands and pulled her toward him.

Panic swept through her. "Please, you're hurting me."

five

Christopher released her abruptly. "I'm sorry. I don't know what's wrong with me."

Audra took several deep breaths to gain control. The moment reminded her too much of the day before with Caleb—when he kissed her with such cruelty.

"Please forgive me," he said.

She nodded, willing her body to cease trembling.

"I'd better go. This is not how a gentleman behaves toward a lady. I can't remember ever being this inconsiderate of a woman."

"I. . .I feel it's too soon for affection."

He looked up into the night sky. "I know I'm deeply distressed about the funeral tomorrow, especially since my brother killed the man. Perhaps I've become no better than he."

She couldn't bear to hear the pain in his voice. "I have to tell you what your brother did. I can't seem to remove it from my mind." She hesitated. "Yesterday, during the robbery, he. . . kissed me. The things he said were cruel."

"Oh, no." Christopher moved closer then stopped. "I want to comfort you, but I shouldn't. I will never disappoint you again, I promise."

She watched his frame slump back to the house. He looked so dejected. "Christopher, God gives us all a new beginning."

He stopped in his stride and turned to face her. "Does that mean you are giving me another chance to prove myself?"

His words sounded like those of a repentant little boy. "I think this is simply the process of getting to know each other."

"My dear Audra, your words are a song from heaven."

❧

Audra raced her horse across the valley to the west of Jed and Naomi's home between their ranch and the Rockies. She marveled at the sun traversing the sky. In a few hours it would dip below the mountains, and the sky would transform from a vivid blue to orange. Her mount was a spirited sorrel mare, and keeping the horse under control took all of her physical strength. But she needed this challenge—a wild attempt to free her mind from the confusion and tragedies of the past few days. The smell of fresh Colorado air and the wind blowing through her tresses ushered in a whisper to trust what she could not see. Her hair eased from the pins at her nape and fell upon her shoulders, and so did the scattered emotions spill from her heart.

Her life had grown out of control in a matter of a few days. The dreams she'd clung to on the journey from Nebraska no longer sustained her. The situation in Earnest begged for deliverance, but what could she do? Pastor Windsor in Nebraska believed his sons pioneered a new country that needed their strength and courage. This horrible situation was like viewing a wasp land on her arm and not knowing whether to shoo it away or wait for it to fly away on its own accord.

She loathed waiting on anything. Patience was a virtue, and she longed for its attributes. If she lacked wisdom, she should ask God. But this dreadful silence told her to trust God. Audra wanted to scream about the unfairness of it all, but instead she galloped across a beautiful, untamed land hoping to find the answers in the midst of God's creation.

This morning she attended the funeral for the driver Caleb killed. His wife sobbed all the way through the service, and his two young daughters took turns trying to comfort her while their liquid grief spilled over their cheeks. The scene at the burial site intensified when someone asked the sheriff when he planned to string up Caleb Windsor. Poor Christopher, caught between God's command to love his brother and the wickedness of his brother's deeds.

As soon as the man was laid to rest, she accompanied Christopher, Papa, and the Masterses to a midday meal at the widow's home. There tempers flew, and the sheriff finally took a posse and left town in search of the murderer. Audra chastised herself for not congratulating the sheriff on his work, but something about the circumstances between Caleb and Christopher bothered her immensely. It came as a feeling—a torment of sorts—and God's bidding to simply refrain from speaking did not help.

Shortly after the meal, she bid Papa good-bye and tearfully watched the stage depart. She prayed it delivered him safely to Denver where he would board the train back to Mama. Papa had not asked her today if she wanted to return, or she'd have agreed.

All the way back to the ranch with Jed and Naomi, she tried to understand her uneasiness. Brothers. One a man of God, the other an outlaw. She likened the situation to Jacob and Esau, possibly Cain and Abel. How had this happened?

The mare beneath her heaved, and Audra slowed the animal's pace. She'd thought about the differences between the brothers for as long as she intended. She'd prayed until her words repeated, and still her heart ached. Beside a clear, bubbling stream that danced over rocks and pushed its way downstream, she dismounted and walked the horse until its breathing slowed.

A bird sang out and the sound combined with the gurgling water. The solace spread a comforter over her misguided world. Allowing the mare to drink freely and graze, she snatched up a bouquet of white-petaled daisies.

"Miss Audra, you ride well."

She whirled around to see a man identical to Christopher standing not twenty feet from her. Gasping, she calculated the time it would take for her to get to the mare.

"There's no need to be afraid," he said, keeping his stance against the backdrop of brush. "Contrary to the rumors, I'm not the evil brother. I won't hurt you."

"Caleb Windsor." The whisper of his name ushered in terror. Alone, helpless, she refused to make him angry. Mama's warnings about the ways of bad men echoed across her mind.

"That is me, but you, like so many others, believe my clever brother."

She covered her mouth and watched the mare drink deeply.

"I did not kill the driver or rob the stage."

"I was there," she said without thinking. "I saw you. How can you deny it?"

"Because the outlaw in the family is Christopher."

She drew in a breath. Lies, all lies.

"If I wanted to harm you, wouldn't I have crossed the distance between us by now? Out here," he said, gesturing, "no one would hear you scream." He leaned on one leg, his voice barely audible above the rushing stream of water. "If I had murdered a man, wouldn't I be on my way to Mexico?"

"Why are you here? Isn't it enough that you killed a man? Hurt my father? Stole my grandmother's brooch and the money Papa and I needed for the trip?"

Anguish ripped across his face. "I have but one purpose—to warn you that your life will be miserable if you marry my brother. He covers his treachery with a cross."

Fury erupted from a fiery pit deep inside her. "Christopher is good and kind. He's tried to stop you, urge you to turn your life over to the Lord."

Caleb chuckled and shook his head. "Let me tell you about my brother. He's always been the selfish one. Then five years ago he figured out how to please folks and rob them at the same time."

His words continued to anger her. She longed to fling dirt on the man. Caleb must be so wretched that he discarded the truth like ragged clothes.

"I have a few questions for you, Miss Audra. Has he won you over with his smooth talk? How often has he prayed with you? Has he pressed you for a wedding date? Has he kissed you without the proper amount of time to pass? Does he grieve his wayward brother in one breath and pledge his support to have me hanged in the next?"

Audra felt herself grow ashen. Caleb didn't know the truth at all. His questions were merely coincidences. Lifting her chin, she stared into his face. "Have you no respect for a man of God?"

"Why not ask him the same question?"

"I wouldn't insult his beliefs or the work he's done for God."

"Remember the letter he wrote your father? I thought Christopher might settle down if he had a wife. I suggested the whole thing, and I've regretted it ever since. It was my idea for you to stay with Jed and Naomi. They're good people, and they know the truth. I suggested he send the money for travel purposes. How ironic, since he stole it back. God forgive me." He paused. "Go on home with your father to Nebraska—to my father's church. Marrying Chris will only fill you with disappointment and sorrow."

"Why should you care?"

"I love my brother, but I've made a terrible mistake by allowing him to use me as a scapegoat—something that started when we were boys. And soon he'll use you. After the killing yesterday, I have to find a way for folks to learn the truth. Robbing was bad enough, but now he's committed murder."

"I don't believe you." Her lips quivered. This had to be a trick.

Caleb walked over to her horse and gathered up the reins. He held them out to her and patted the mare on the neck. "Time will tell the truth," he said. "Don't let him convince you to stay at the boardinghouse, because there you won't learn the truth until it is too late." He smiled, so much like Christopher that she shuddered. "Best you head on back to Jed and Naomi's before dusk. I wouldn't want the sheriff's men to mistake you for me."

Shaking, she took the reins and lifted herself onto the horse.

For a moment she felt a twinge of embarrassment at not riding sidesaddle, but her emotions were already stretched.

"Look at me," Caleb said.

Fearful of disobeying him, she stared into his face. The same face of the man of God who wanted her to be his wife and share in his ministry.

"Study every feature about me, Miss Audra. Remember my eyes and the tone of my voice. I am not the man you think I am. Ask God to show you the truth." With those words, he turned and walked away.

All the way back to the ranch, she pondered Caleb and the strange encounter. As the sun sank lower behind her, so did her spirits. Her mind seemed swollen with questions. His final statement bothered her the most. *Study every feature about me, Miss Audra. Remember my eyes and the tone of my voice. I am not the man you think I am. Ask God to show you the truth.*

Yes, Lord, show me the truth. Do I speak to Jed and Naomi? Or do I make observations on my own?

The Windsor brother who had robbed the stage did not in the least resemble the Caleb Windsor she met today.

Audra decided not to say anything to Jed and Naomi about meeting Caleb. Every word and gesture stayed fixed in her thoughts. She'd always prided herself in being a good judge of character, but confusion over who to trust clouded her every twist and turn. Even considering Christopher might be the real outlaw seemed incredulous—and moved her to ask forgiveness. Caleb wanted to taint his brother's ministry, and she would not fall into his horrible plan.

Certain the man she met on Jed and Naomi's ranch was Satan in disguise, she planned to tell Christopher as soon as he visited again. The following morning while she helped Naomi finish the last of the weekly washing, Christopher rode up on a dark chestnut gelding. He didn't look at all like a pastor, but more like a ranch hand, rugged and appealing, very appealing.

"Morning, Mrs. Masters, Miss Audra." He leaned on the

saddle horn and tipped his hat. "How are you ladies this fine day?"

Naomi turned with one of Jed's shirts in hand. "Just working, Pastor. Trying to keep a step ahead of my ornery husband."

"I suspect you've been working on that little project for a lot of years."

Naomi laughed. "I suppose so. What brings you out here? I'm sure it's not to spend the day teasing an old woman."

"To see you, of course, and say hello to Miss Audra."

"More likely the latter." She gestured at Audra. "Watch this man, Audra. Rumor is he's looking for a wife."

Caleb's words stole across her mind like a throbbing headache. She instantly pushed them away. Smoothing a borrowed apron over her black skirt, she caught Christopher's gaze and felt her cheeks warm.

"Maybe I've found one." Christopher grinned and threw his leg over his horse. "When Miss Audra finishes helping you, could she be excused for a walk?"

"We're done now, Pastor. And why don't you ask her?" Naomi placed her hands on her ample hips and nodded at Audra. "Go ahead, dear."

Audra and Christopher strolled in the direction of the corral where a ranch hand attempted to saddle a stallion. The horse jumped and snorted, its ears laid back in obvious rebellion.

"Have you forgiven me?" Christopher asked.

"Yes. I haven't given it another thought." Too many other matters had taken over the near kiss—such as his brother.

"Thank you. I've been so angry with myself that I haven't been able to concentrate on this Sunday's sermon."

"Then put your worries aside and concentrate on God's calling."

He watched the stallion throw the ranch hand into the dirt. "Thank you, Audra. Not a moment has passed that I haven't regretted my actions that night. I needed horsewhipped."

She laughed and relaxed slightly. "I think not." She paused. "I would like to tell you something."

He lifted a brow and for a moment she considered the matter with Caleb unimportant, but now was not the time to start keeping things from her husband—or husband to be. "I met Caleb again."

Christopher's features hardened, and his body stiffened. "Did he try to hurt you?"

"No, he was too busy warning me about you." Audra swallowed hard and forced herself to peer into his face.

"Warn you about me? I don't understand."

"He said you were really the outlaw and that he'd always taken the blame for your actions."

He pounded his fist onto the fence rail. "How dare he? He must have gone mad. Audra, I'm afraid for you. Where did you see him?"

"I'd gone riding."

"Riding?"

Why did she feel as though she'd done something wrong? "I needed to get away, to—"

"By yourself?"

"Why are you angry with me?"

"Audra, this is not safe country. Please do not leave the ranch without an escort. It's too dangerous."

"All right. I simply wanted time alone."

"Until Caleb is found, you'll have to forgo such pleasures." His tone grew tender. "I worry about you. Perhaps you should consider taking a room at the boardinghouse where I can watch out for you."

Caleb's words haunted her again. "I'll be careful. I do enjoy staying here with Jed and Naomi."

"But what if Caleb shows up here. . .harms you or them?" He pressed his lips together as though he wanted to say more but thought better of it. "Please, Audra, if you lived in town, I would know that you were safe."

Lines deepened across his forehead, reminding her of Papa's plowed fields. "I'll think about it." Christopher had enough on his mind without her adding to his problems.

"If you must go riding, then we can ride together."
Christopher's face softened. "I promised your father I would
take good care of you."

six

Caleb waited at the top of a pine-covered ridge where he knew his brother would pass by on his way to town. He'd seen Christopher head toward the Masterses' ranch earlier and figured he went to pay Audra a call. Caleb followed. He crept on foot close enough to observe his brother draw Audra aside to talk. From the look on Chris's face, he was doing his best to convince her of his sincerity. How often had he seen his brother twist an ounce of truth into a wagonload of lies? The thought made him want to stomp up to the corral fence and lay his fist alongside Chris's jaw. A whole lot of good that would do. He could imagine Audra screaming for help and Chris accusing him of every crime this side of the mountains. Any credibility Caleb might have garnered in meeting with Audra would sift through his fingers like fine dirt.

Still the thought gave Caleb immense satisfaction. He continued to watch the two and, from his vantage point, he saw the expressions on Audra's face as well. At first she appeared stubborn, even defiant, but Chris eventually won her over. The peaceful, sweet glances from her told Caleb all he suspected was true.

For a moment he allowed himself to dwell on his first meeting with Audra. Although she'd appeared frightened of him, she'd displayed such courage. And up close she was more beautiful than ever.

Now Caleb sat atop his horse and kept his focus on the road for signs of his no-account brother. One more time he'd attempt to talk some sense into him. A bird flew overhead, and the sun warmed his back. In the distance he saw angry gray clouds gather and move his way. He expelled a heavy sigh. From the looks of nature, he'd be sleeping in Jed's barn again instead of under a star-studded sky. Since the wanted posters went up months ago, he couldn't ride within ten feet of his own place. Some days he wondered if his own men might shoot him for the reward, to say nothing of the sheriff's men or a hungry bounty hunter.

God, when will this end? Chris has to stop robbing from folks, and I need to clear my name.

Silence, always silence. Every word and action from Caleb worked toward justice and truth, and he prayed God rode ahead of him to pave the way. Like the storm brewing in the distance, he feared he'd be caught without shelter when it all came pouring down.

The sound of hoof beats rhythmically pounding against the road alerted Caleb to a rider. He moved out from the wooded refuge to take a look. Chris rode at breakneck speed, a man in too big a hurry. Caleb planted his horse in the middle of the road. No matter where his brother headed, he was going to listen to reason today.

"Get out of my way," Chris shouted. "I'm late."

"I don't care if you never get to where you're going," Caleb said. "We're going to talk."

Chris slowed his horse when Caleb refused to move. "What's this all about?"

"Murder, robbery, and Audra Lenders."

Chris laughed. "Guilty as charged. What are you going to do about it?"

Caleb fought the rage brewing inside him like the fast approaching storm. "Stop you, if I die trying."

"And you might do just that." Chris's words stung with the seriousness of the problems between them.

"Has it come to killing your own brother?" Caleb asked.

"You're the one who said you would stop me or die trying."

Caleb sized up his twin, identical in looks but never in mind and heart. "I'm talking jail."

"And what do you think the law will do with a man convicted of murder?"

"That's for a court to decide."

Chris cursed. "I need to check on my horses. Move out of my way."

"Not until we get a few things settled." Caleb tried again to control his anger, but it walked two paces ahead of him. He swallowed hard and caught a glimpse of a patch of sunlight not yet covered by the gray clouds. Hope. God always offered His light. "Brother, you think more of your horses than you do people, and I admit you take fine care of them. But I want you to turn yourself in before it gets worse. There are folks who will vouch for me, clear my name."

"And there are a whole lot more who'll string you up."

"Those are my terms. I give you three days to confess to the sheriff. In the meantime, you leave Miss Lenders alone."

Again Chris laughed. "She's too pretty to leave alone. I know you've noticed. And for your information, I have plans to leave Colorado."

"When?"

"Got me just about enough money to head south for Mexico. I plan on cashing in on my hard work in about six weeks," Chris said.

"That's too long. Three days, like I said before."

"Forget it. I'll do as I please." Chris pulled his horse around Caleb. "I will marry Audra as planned then leave her here."

"Haven't you done enough? I can't stand by and not try to stop you."

"I won't let you. I'm faking my death, and you'll still be on the run." With those words, Chris took off toward Earnest.

Only his faith in God stopped Caleb from going after his brother. The truth was he wanted to pound some sense into him, and he'd most likely hurt Chris a whole lot more than he intended.

The law had ways of handling men like Christopher Windsor. Caleb simply hated the thought of his brother serving time in a rat-infested prison—or worse. Caleb had always looked out for his brother. Chris had been sickly when they were little boys, and the woman who took care of him never seemed to give the love he craved. Maybe a mother's love would have made a difference, and Chris wouldn't have tried so hard to get folks to notice him.

The storm clouds moved faster than Caleb anticipated. He rode toward the Masterses' ranch. He needed to confront Miss Audra about a few things.

❧

Audra helped Naomi put dinner on the table. Mealtimes were a rush of activity until food was delivered to the ranch hands at the bunkhouse. Those men inhaled their food like they'd never eaten before. Nearly made Audra sick. The storm made things worse as rain threatened to ruin the ham and beans and a huge mound of cornbread with butter and honey. Audra, covered in a parka that belonged to Jed, carried the coffeepot in one hand and a crock jug of buttermilk in the other. A flash of lightning and an ear-piercing crack of thunder caused her nearly to drop both. Once inside the bunkhouse and the food delivered to the three hands, Naomi announced her readiness to step back out in the rain.

"Is it wrong to pray for this to ease up?" Audra asked as the rain sliced against the window and another bellow of thunder shook the bunkhouse.

"If it is, then I'm guilty," Naomi said. "Let's go, Audra. Never let it be said this old woman was afraid of a little bad weather."

With Naomi's round body swishing ahead of her, Audra followed like an obedient chick after its mama. She imagined the ranch hands were chuckling at the sight of the two women dashing across the mud-ridden path. A flash of lightning that caused her hair to stand on end made her glad she didn't need to visit the outhouse. She half expected the necessary building to go up in flames at any moment.

Once safe inside the house, she realized she'd been holding her breath. The powerful display of nature reminded her of the storms at home in Nebraska. She'd dreaded them, too.

"All that excitement has made me hungry," Naomi said. "As soon as Jed gets in, we'll eat. Don't you know those men were laughing at us?"

Audra laughed. "I thought the same thing." She hung both parkas on pegs and watched them drip onto the floor. She then set two bowls beneath them to catch the water. "Naomi, despite this nasty weather, I enjoy every minute here with you and Jed."

"Well, thank you. We love having you here, too."

She remembered Christopher urging her to move into town. The thought of ever leaving the Masterses saddened her. As soon as supper rested on the table, the door opened, and Jed stepped inside with a man behind him.

"Good to see you, Caleb," Naomi said. "Got plenty of ham and beans here."

Audra gasped. Why, it was as though Caleb often came to see them.

"Thank you, Ma." He kissed the woman's cheek. "I hate my own cooking."

Jed chuckled. "I'd be the size of a fencepost if it weren't for her feeding me so good."

Naomi nodded at Audra. "I need to introduce our guest."

"We. . .we've met," Audra said. Christopher would be so upset.

Caleb touched the brim of his rain-soaked hat. "Evenin', Miss Lenders."

Audra met his gaze, mostly out of defiance, but warmth stared back at her. Confused, she busied herself in setting another place for the outlaw. A flurry of questions assaulted her. Why were Jed and Naomi so friendly with Caleb? Were they afraid of what he might do? Were they outlaws, too? Didn't they understand this man cared for no one but himself?

"Caleb is a regular visitor," Jed said as though reading her thoughts. "He's a fine man—not what others think."

Audra swallowed hard and failed to comment. Frightened best described her.

"You can sit down now," Naomi said. "We have plenty of time to discuss the Windsor brothers and the horrible mess Christopher has made of things." She bent her head for Jed's blessing of the food, but Audra couldn't concentrate.

The others ate heartily. Rather than make her uneasiness evident, Audra picked at her food and shoved it around on her plate to make it look like she was eating. Meanwhile, Naomi, Jed, and Caleb talked about everything but what screamed through Audra's mind.

"I do have a purpose for being here tonight." Caleb scooped up another slice of cornbread and reached for the pitcher of honey. He glanced up at Audra. "I met with Chris after I saw him talk to Miss Lenders this afternoon."

Audra trembled and placed her fork beside her plate. He'd been spying on them? "Perhaps you should spend more time following what the pastor says."

Jed coughed and reached for his coffee. With a deep breath, he managed to speak. "If we kept better track of the good pastor, we could have avoided a funeral."

"Pardon me, Mr. Masters, but aren't you confused?" Audra asked.

Silence permeated the room, interrupted only by the falling rain outside.

Naomi touched Audra's arm. "Honey, there's a lot you don't know, and I've been meaning to tell you. Guess I knew how badly the news would upset you."

"I've told her already," Caleb said. "But she doesn't believe a word of it. Chris has done a fine job."

Naomi placed her napkin in her lap. "What's happened now?"

"I told him today that I intended to stop him and that he had three days to turn himself in to the sheriff." Caleb pushed back his plate. "He didn't take kindly to it and gave me a little advance notice of his plans."

Jed rubbed his face. "It's all I can do to tolerate the sound of his voice on Wednesday nights and Sundays. Pretending to like him don't make me feel any better about myself either. Go ahead and tell us, son. What's he intendin' to do?"

Audra peered into Caleb's face, not sure if she wanted to hear another lie or not. To think her dear new friends had fallen under his spell. She studied his face. He was a good one at deceiving folks. If she didn't know better, she'd swear he knew Jesus.

"He says he has almost enough money to head to Mexico."

"That's a relief," Naomi said.

"Not really. He intends to follow through with courtin' and marrying Miss Lenders then fake his death. That way the law will still be after me."

"Oh, no." Huge tears slid down Naomi's cheeks. "I know I've asked this before, but why, Caleb? From what you've told me about your father, he's a fine man who did his best to raise you boys right."

Caleb nodded. "He loved us and taught us right from wrong. His congregation kept him busy, but he always found time for us. The truth is, if I hadn't covered up for Chris all these years, he might not be the thief and murderer he is today."

"Don't go blaming yourself. He made his own choices." Jed turned to Audra. "I see in your face that you're doubtin' what we're saying, so I'm asking you to take what we say to the Lord. He'll give you the truth."

She intended to do that very thing. "Yes, sir. Christopher took good care of Papa and has been kind to me. I find this very hard to believe."

"He paid for your father's return home, right?" Jed asked. When she nodded he continued. "The money Chris used was probably the same that he stole from you. Now how do you feel about his generosity?"

Audra said nothing. *Lord, help me. They sound so convincing, but Christopher couldn't possibly be an outlaw, could he?*

"Do you understand if Chris follows through with what he's planning, he will never face his crimes?" Jed asked. "And Caleb will still be a wanted man."

"And you," Naomi sighed and dabbed at her eyes, "might be left with a child to raise by yourself. If you did find another husband, you'd be married to two men at the same time."

Audra stood from the table. Her cheeks flushed hot at Naomi's intimate suggestion. Why ever did Christopher bring her to these people's home?

"Miss Lenders, please sit down," Caleb said. "No one here wants to hurt you. No one has anything to gain by telling you all this. We're warning you, that's all. Do what Jed says. Pray about my brother—and think real hard about going home to Nebraska."

❧

Caleb lay awake in Jed's barn, bone-tired and worn out from feuding with Chris. Every time he considered what to do about his brother, the plan exploded in his face. The one he had now didn't look much better. Chris had to be caught in a crime while posing as the town's pastor. But how? Tomorrow he'd talk to Jed and Naomi about it. Between the three of them, God would surely give them an answer.

Audra kept stepping into his thoughts. Besides being the prettiest woman he'd ever seen, she had an admirable strength about her. Beneath those pale blue eyes shimmering like the sun on a patch of wildflowers, he saw true inner beauty. At first he hated the fact she didn't believe the truth about Christopher, but when he pondered on it, he found her trait commendable. She wasn't easily persuaded once she had her mind fixed on something. But her determination also meant when she finally realized the true outlaw, she'd be madder than an agitated nest of hornets.

Tonight, he wondered if he'd ever meet a woman like Audra Lenders again. He'd given up on having a wife and family, but after being around her tonight, he suddenly yearned for those things again. *Am I being a fool, Lord? I'm actually jealous of my brother. Coveting is a sin, and I know it, but isn't this situation different?*

Tossing and turning on the straw pallet, Caleb listened to

the rain and decided he'd best be gone before Audra woke. Seeing her again with another one of her loathing stares would make him feel less than a man.

seven

"Isn't this glorious?" Audra asked. "I love Colorado—everything about it. The fresh air, the green mountains, all these beautiful wildflowers, the blue mountains in the distance with the white peaks, and a place to stay that is not a smelly soddy."

Christopher laughed. They'd stopped their horses to gaze out over the valley where Jed and Naomi's horses and cattle pastured. "Shall I move my church out here?"

She swung her attention his way with a sudden fierce devotion to this man. How handsome he looked sitting erect in the saddle and peering at her with a mixture of humor and admiration. "Could you?" A lopsided grin met her, and she realized the foolishness of her question. "Guess the ride from town might be a problem for some, and this is Jed and Naomi's land."

"Yes, my dear Audra. A church here would not be wise. Its location in Earnest suits God's purpose."

At times she detested practicality. A fantasy world appealed to her today, one with no worries about tomorrow.

"You look so serious," he said. "What has put such a frown on your pretty face?"

She took in a breath and admired the sunlight haloing his head. "Wanting desperately for everything to be perfect, and yet knowing it is impossible."

"I believe every good thing in life is for the taking."

The peculiar remark from a man of God begged for an explanation. "What do you mean? I thought love and obedience brought God's blessings. I'm not sure if we are to take things."

"We are speaking the same. I used the word *taking* instead

of blessings or gifts. God wants us to have all the good things of life."

"I think I understand." Audra needed to meditate on his words later when she didn't have his wonderful company to distract her.

"Shall we lead the horses for a while?

"I'd like that." A breeze picked up a few stray tendrils and tickled her neck. They walked in silence. Every sight and sound of nature welcomed the promise of summer.

"Has my brother frightened you anymore?"

She recalled two nights ago and Caleb's presence at supper. "No, he hasn't said or done anything to make me afraid." *Irritated and angry best describes my feelings about your brother's ridiculous claims.*

"Good. I've decided to denounce his activities at tomorrow morning's service and encourage the men to help the sheriff." He paused and managed what looked like a difficult swallow. No doubt his emotions about Caleb cut at his heart. "I'm fearful folks think I know his whereabouts, which is quite the contrary." He sighed. "The incident that happened after I left you at the Masterses' made folks angrier. The sheriff has to find my brother before anyone else is killed." He blinked and glanced away in the distance. "This is so hard, Audra. My own flesh and blood an outlaw."

"What happened?" She wondered if Christopher had learned that Caleb had been at the ranch. He'd stayed way into the night talking to Jed.

"While folks east of town were eating their supper, Caleb and his men stole thirty head of cattle. One of the ranch hands saw him and his gang."

"East of town?" *Impossible. How could Caleb be rustling cattle and eating with us at the same time?* A shiver snaked up her spine.

"Are you sure?" When Christopher stared at her oddly, she caught her breath. "I mean how could he be so brazen shortly after the stagecoach robbery?"

"I don't think my brother thinks about a proper length of time before he steps out again with his gang. He has a taste for blood and power, and it grows worse."

She paled at the impact of his words. Who told the truth? Confusion twisted at her stomach.

"Oh, forgive me for frightening you. You have no idea how Caleb can manipulate people."

Audra bit her tongue to keep from stating what she knew about Caleb's friendship with Jed and Naomi. An inner urging stopped her, and she'd always been sensitive to God curbing her tongue—even if she didn't always listen. "The crimes must end, Christopher, although the cost of losing your brother is a high price."

Sadness swept over his features. "I lost him a long time ago. I have nightmares of conducting his funeral." He wrapped the horse's reins around a tree then took hers and did the same. "I believe I've been blessed with you, Audra. You will be my ray of light in all of this gloom. Let's talk of more pleasant things, like you and me."

"That is much more agreeable," she said.

A moment later the two strolled side by side while their horses grazed on the new tender grass. She thought of Mama and Papa. When she left Nebraska, she didn't think she'd ever pine away for them, but in these turbulent times she missed them sorely.

"What must I do to convince you of my love?" Boyish innocence ushered in a glimpse of Christopher's heart.

"This soon? We barely have grown beyond our given names." Audra noted a strange sensation clawing at her heart.

"I felt you and I were handpicked by God the first time I set eyes on you. I truly felt an angel stepped down from the stage." He gathered her hands into his and bent closer. "Don't you feel the same? I can think of no one else that I'd rather have beside me for the rest of my life than you, Audra Lenders. Together we can do God's work and build a family of our own. I love you more with every passing moment."

Her pulse quickened at his declaration. A flame burned in his eyes, one that unnerved her. "Oh, Christopher, you invite such dreams into my heart. I think if not for this horrible tragedy of your brother, I'd say yes this very minute."

He drew her closer, and she went willingly, but the force of his grip intensified the panic she'd sensed earlier. "I can take care of Caleb. We shouldn't let anything stand in the way of our happiness."

His grip tightened, and she trembled. "Christopher, you frighten me. Please let me go."

"Don't you think a man has the right to hold his future bride and taste her lips?"

She stared into his eyes. The look he offered spoke of matters intended for a husband and wife. "Take me back to the house. I'm uncomfortable."

Christopher's fingers tightened around her wrist. "Did you think that you could tempt me with your presence out here away from everyone and say no to my affections? How cruel for one who proclaims innocence."

Audra struggled. "I had no such idea at all. Please, Christopher."

His head bent lower and his hot breath sent tremors up and down her spine.

An unseen hand pulled him away from her. "Leave her alone, Chris."

She gasped. Caleb Windsor had come to her aid?

Christopher released Audra and turned to swing at Caleb, but Caleb stopped the blow and held Christopher back. "I told you before to leave her alone."

"She is none of your business." Christopher shook off Caleb's hold.

"And I told you that I was going to stop what you're doing. I will defend anyone you attempt to abuse."

"You can't be everywhere. I have plans and nobody is getting in my way."

Caleb narrowed his gaze. "Keep going, Chris, and you're

going to hang yourself."

"I don't think so. You're the one wanted for murder and robbery."

Audra stared incredulously. The words flying between the two brothers almost sounded as though Caleb had been right.

Caleb grabbed Christopher by the collar. "I gave you three days, and this is day two. Turn yourself in to the sheriff, or I'm handling it."

Christopher laughed. "I'm the respected Windsor in the community, or have you forgotten?"

Caleb glanced at Audra. "She's listening to every word."

"And what does that mean? Audra and I plan to marry as soon as the law catches up to you—possibly sooner. We may have our differences, but misunderstandings have nothing to do with our love."

Caleb stepped back from his brother. "You know about love? Animals are more respectful of each other than you are." He whirled around to her. "Miss Audra, once I asked you to remember everything about me. Now I'm asking you to remember every word that has passed between Chris and me here today. Think on it. And think on what might have happened if I hadn't been here."

Audra chose not to trust the words of either man. Right now she wanted to be in the security of Jed and Naomi's home. "I'm riding back to the house."

"I'll go with you," Christopher said. "I need to explain."

Audra glared at him, fists clenched. "I'd rather be alone."

"I'll escort you," Caleb said. "I have my horse behind those trees."

"I said I'd rather ride alone, thank you."

"I understand, Miss Audra, but I intend to accompany you until you're safely at Jed and Naomi's." Caleb turned to a clump of trees, and she hurried away to her horse.

"Audra, wait," Christopher called. "All right, believe that lawless brother of mine. He's going to swing for all he's done."

She picked up her pace, not once giving a Windsor

brother her attention. "I don't believe or trust either of you."
Once Audra reached the tree where her horse stood waiting,
she swung up into the saddle only to find Caleb riding up
beside her. Every muscle and nerve stiffened. He wasn't riding the pewter-colored stallion but a dark brown mare.

They rode in silence. She considered spurring on her horse,
but in truth she needed the solace to pray through what had
happened. Christopher's harshness when she refused his kiss
shook her more than the twister that carried off the roof of
the soddy back in Nebraska. And this wasn't the first time.
What she'd learned from Mama about men and what she'd
observed from the young men back home had no resemblance
to her experience with Christopher. It seemed as though he
turned into another man when they were alone, one who
frightened her.

Feigning interest in the countryside, she cast a sideways
glance at Caleb. He'd come to her rescue, as though he suspected Christopher's behavior. She still trembled and fought
to gain control. Uncertainty etched her mind, a state she'd felt
more than once lately. Why would an outlaw want to help
her? What did Caleb and Christopher's conversation mean?

"Why don't you tell me what you're thinking? Might help
to sort things out," Caleb said.

Audra wished she could cry, but those sentiments didn't
solve a thing. Taking a deep breath, she tightened her fingers
around the reins. "Why aren't you riding the pewter-colored
stallion?"

He shook his head. "Don't own one. A horse fitting that
description belongs to Chris."

A shiver danced up and down her arms. "Do you ever
ride it?"

"It's a one-man horse. High-spirited. I have my own." He
stopped in the middle of the path and pushed back his hat, a
tan color with a short crown. His dark hair fell across his
collar, a little longer than Christopher's. "Keep remembering
things, Miss Audra. You'll figure out the truth."

She stared at her gloved hands. "The man who held up the stage rode a pewter-colored stallion."

"I know." He urged his horse forward.

"He also wore a dark brown hat with a high crown."

"I'm wearing my only hat." He expelled a heavy sigh. "Chris will have an excuse for today. Probably will tell you he's unworthy of you and beg forgiveness."

"He should say those things. His behavior was uncalled for."

"Always is."

"Are you saying there is nothing good about Christopher?"

Caleb shrugged and took a deep breath. "He loves that horse. We used to have an old dog he liked. He'd do about anything to please our father. Tell you what, Chris is good with horses. Takes care of them like they were his children. He's clean and neat. When he makes up his mind about something, he doesn't give up."

"Even to be a pastor?"

Caleb's gaze didn't waver. "Even to be a pastor."

"What about you? You say you aren't the outlaw, but how did all of this start?"

He pressed his lips together then moistened them as though he tasted something vile. "Chris spent a lot of time sick when we were younger, and I felt sorry for him. He's always been the rebellious one, had a habit of venturing one step farther than what was right. I hated to see him get punished all the time, so as a kid I started admitting to things I didn't do. That way both of us looked like we were headed for big trouble instead of Chris. As we grew up, I covered for him until I looked like the worst one." Caleb stopped to watch a buck and two deer nibble at some grass to the right of them. "We came out here with the idea of leaving the past behind. Both of us wanted to go into ranching. Soon after, Chris got mixed up with bad company. We argued, then he decided he wanted to pastor a church. We argued about that too, 'cause I knew God hadn't called him. Anyway, about two years ago he started rustling cattle and horses. Somebody saw him, and I got the blame. Nothing's changed since we were boys."

"And you're telling me he's done all of these crimes and covered for himself by being a pastor?" Audra had heard children tell bigger tales than this.

"Yes, ma'am. In a way it's my fault. I started the problem a long time ago."

The even tone of his voice rang with confidence. Doubts crept in like slow rising water. Today the roles of the men seemed reversed.

"Why did you help me?" she asked. *If you are the real outlaw, you had no difficulty stealing a kiss by force.*

"I made a decision to stop Chris, right after he shot the driver." He pointed to an eagle soaring overhead, a magnificent creature with its proud white head and golden beak. The regal bird appeared to guard the earth below. "Besides, you're a lovely lady, Audra Lenders. Naomi tells me your heart is pure gold. She cares for you like a daughter, and you love Jesus."

She held her hat and watched the eagle circle above them. *Oh, Lord, I don't understand what is going on.* Her head ached from trying to discern the truth. "If Christopher has stolen all these things, where are they?"

Caleb said nothing for several moments. "I have no idea where he's hidden them. I've searched the area for miles around looking for the cattle and horses, but I imagine they're already wearing another brand and headed south to sell."

"Where is your ranch?"

He pointed northeast. "I have a good foreman who runs things for me. The sheriff has combed every inch of it and inspected my cattle and horses more times than I can count."

Could he be telling the truth? She relived the angry words Christopher and Caleb threw at each other.

"So now you believe me?" he asked.

She turned away. "I didn't say that at all. Honestly, neither of you measures up to your father."

Audra dug her heels into her horse and raced the remaining distance to the ranch, leaving Caleb in a flurry of dust and dirt. What an outlandish story. The two men deserved each other, the outlaw and the demanding pastor.

She caught her breath. Caleb couldn't have been two places at the same time. Could the ranch owner have lied to Christopher about his brother's actions? That didn't make sense.

Why did Caleb have more manners than Christopher?

Why did Christopher behave like a spoiled child?

Why hadn't she listened to Mama and stayed in Nebraska?

❧

Caleb skirted the hill overlooking the Masters' ranch. He expected Christopher to ride in there to make amends with Miss Audra, but he hadn't crossed this way. That woman could charm the honey from a nest of bees. Each time he saw her, his insides turned to apple butter. The way he looked at it, any man would be proud to have Audra Lenders as a bride. Why, he'd gladly spend the rest of his life making sure she wore a smile every day. He hoped she learned the truth soon, because he'd like the chance to win her.

Tomorrow was Sunday, the third day of Chris's deadline to turn himself in. One of Chris's men offered to come forward when he'd been cheated out of his share of a robbery. Caleb had arranged to meet him Monday morning at the Masters' ranch. Then they'd head into town to meet with the sheriff. With Jed and Naomi planning to testify, Chris should be in jail come mid afternoon.

He hated doing this to their father, but he had no choice. The killings and robberies had to end.

eight

Audra paced the kitchen floor with the anticipation that Christopher planned to ride out to the ranch and apologize. Her gaze rested on Naomi's largest iron skillet as the older woman stood cleaning it before she fried chicken. He'd best take his sweet talk elsewhere, or she just might use that skillet on him. She didn't want to hear about his remorse or blame his imprudent behavior on her charms. When she stopped to think about it, no young man in Nebraska ever treated her with such disrespect, and he called himself a man of God. Maybe Caleb and the Masterses had spoken the truth—or both of the Windsor twins were a downright disgrace to their father.

She allotted time for the brothers to quarrel, even throw a few punches, but neither man showed his face.

"Just as well," she said louder than she intended.

Naomi dropped the iron skillet, and Audra startled. "What happened out there with Christopher?"

Audra crossed her arms. "Christopher *and* Caleb. The good pastor needs to work on his manners, and Caleb. . .and Caleb. . ."

"Caleb what?"

She shook her head and halted in the middle of the floor. "He's supposed to be an outlaw, but he has this habit of rescuing me when Christopher. . ."

"Christopher what?"

Audra dug her fingernails into her upper arms. "He can be aggressive."

"Most outlaws are."

"Unlike you and Jed, I'm not convinced that Christopher is the outlaw." She sounded too much like a whining toddler.

64

"Whatever happened to the simple life when a person could tell right off who were the law-biding folks and who were not?"

"My dear, you moved to Colorado and met the Windsor twins." Naomi's tone held a frankness guaranteed to pry loose the cobwebs in Audra's mind, the ones that demanded an explanation of what was really happening in Earnest. "Caleb made mistakes by covering up for his brother, but he's long since seen the result of his decisions. Loving someone doesn't mean you shelter them from their own wrongdoing. All of us have to learn right from wrong by facing the consequences of our actions."

Audra sank into a chair. The anger had vanished, but in its place rested more doubts about Pastor Christopher Windsor. She swallowed hard and remembered. . .

"Some of the things Christopher said didn't sound like a pastor." She paused. "His ambiguous remarks made me angry. I didn't see a reason for it—like he was arguing with Caleb about one thing but wanting me to believe another."

"Tell me more so I can help you." Naomi took a chair beside her.

"He said Caleb stole thirty head of cattle, but he was here when the rustling took place."

"That's not the first time Caleb's been accused of a crime while he was with Jed and me."

"There's more. He said he had plans, and I don't think he meant God's work. Now I wonder if you and Jed have spoken the truth all along."

There, she said it. Her stomach fluttered—not in fear or sickness, but with realization. The certainty of who was the good man and who was the vile one suddenly became as clear as a mountain spring. Only God could touch her with the truth and leave her feeling convinced. She lifted her gaze to Naomi; a tear trickled down the older woman's face.

"I believe you just answered the question tormenting your mind," Naomi said. "Or rather, God revealed whom to believe."

Audra swallowed. "I have to be absolutely sure. I'm sorry. Accusing a pastor of murder?" She paused to gather her wits. "Do you know Christopher and Caleb's middle names?"

Naomi tilted her head. Confusion etched her brow. "Yes. It's Caleb Andrew and Christopher Wesley."

Audra held her breath and covered her mouth. "The man who held up the stagecoach used a folded, clean handkerchief with the initials CWW to wipe blood from my hand." She moistened her lips. "How could one man pose as a man of God and commit those horrible crimes?" She rose from the chair. Understanding sickened her. "Naomi, he shot and killed that man, comforted his widow and daughters, and then preached at his funeral. Is he mad? He even encouraged the men in his congregation to go after Caleb." Whipping her attention to the older woman, Audra felt herself grow pale. "Why am I saying this? You've known the truth all along."

Naomi gathered up Audra's hands. "At times I've wanted to stand up in the middle of church and shake my fist at him. And Jed? Oh my, if he ever unleashes his temper on that young man, there won't be any place where Christopher Windsor can hide."

"What can we do? I know tomorrow is the third day when Caleb said he'd turn over evidence to the sheriff."

"Do you honestly think the sheriff will believe Caleb? Would you, if you hadn't seen for yourself?"

Audra gazed at Naomi solemnly. "Caleb will get himself killed."

"Jed is going to try and talk some sense into him this evening. Caleb's intentions are noble, but if he's killed, Christopher will find another way to continue breaking the law. There must be another way to prove Caleb's innocence."

Audra deliberated the problem. No man should be punished for something he didn't do. And a guilty man shouldn't go free either. Not that she cared much for Caleb. "Mama and Papa were right. I should have stayed in Nebraska," she said. "Then I wouldn't be in this fix."

"But Caleb would still have this problem." Naomi shrugged. "I care for that young man, and I'm probably selfish here, but God may have had a reason for bringing you here—to help him clear his name."

"Me?"

"Yes, my dear. If anyone in these parts can find out information about Christopher, you can."

"He won't tell me a thing after today."

A slow grin spread over Naomi's face. "What if you went to him and said you had made a mistake? Asked him to give you another chance?"

"Lie? I can't do that!"

The older woman cringed. "I don't believe in lying either. When I think about it, Jed and I have been living a lie to protect Caleb."

"I want to help, but I'm not sure how." The seriousness of the situation settled on her like the heavy air before a storm.

"I suggest you pray about what to do. This isn't your battle anyway, and I was wrong in asking you to put yourself in harm's way."

Audra wrapped her arm around Naomi's round shoulder. "This became my battle when I saw a man killed, attended his funeral, and comforted his wife and daughters. When I think of poor Belle raising those little girls by herself, I want to take a switch to Christopher. Who will be next?"

❧

Caleb spotted Jed riding his way. He expected him. No doubt his old friend wanted to talk him out of going to the sheriff tomorrow. But he'd made up his mind. He'd rather risk arrest and conviction than allow his brother to break one more law. Having a witness should help, too, even if the man had once ridden with Chris. With the killing and plans to leave the country, no telling what his brother would do next. He hated what the news would do to their father. He'd been so proud of Christopher entering the ministry. Now their father would learn not only how Caleb had taken the blame all these years for Chris but also how he'd written the letter for Miss Audra to come to Earnest.

Jed waved and rode closer. For a stout man, he handled himself well on a horse, and his age hadn't slowed him down on the ranch either. "I've been looking all over for you," Jed said.

Caleb grinned. "Now you found me. Sure glad you're not a lawman."

"Aren't you the lucky one? We need to talk, and Naomi wants you to come for dinner."

"As if I might be stupid enough to refuse her cooking?"

"Then come with me, and we can talk along the way."

Caleb mounted his horse, mentally calculating when Jed would start in about heading to the sheriff tomorrow morning.

"We've had a good bit of rain this month. The grass is growing up thick and green," Jed said.

"Yes, it is." Caleb laughed inwardly.

"The new calves will fatten up just fine. I might even make a little money this year. Wouldn't you like to ride across your own land and not worry about gettin' shot or hanged?"

Caleb inhaled deeply. "That's what I'm taking care of tomorrow."

"Isn't your witness an outlaw?"

"Used to be."

"Correction, he's still wanted by the law. So who's the sheriff going to believe, an outlaw or the town's preacher?"

"I have to try." An icy chill raced up Caleb's arms, despite the warm temperature.

"Then try smart. God love you, son, but when it comes to your brother you haven't a lick of sense. Do you think he's going to confess when he's already asked men in the church to gun you down?"

"I don't think he'd really go through with it."

Jed reined in his horse. "He doesn't have to. Some bounty hunter or lawman will do it for him."

As usual Jed pointed out the logical side of things. The

truth be known, Caleb was tired of fighting his brother. He was a prisoner as surely as if he lived behind bars. He didn't want his brother hanged or sentenced to life in prison. He simply wanted him stopped. *I am a fool when it comes to my brother. He has to face a judge and jury for what he's done.*

"Most likely seeing you dead wouldn't put an end to things. He'd find another way to cheat folks." Jed's words spoke Caleb's thoughts.

"Then what do you think I should do?"

"Like I said." Jed lifted his reins and urged his horse to walk. "Come to dinner. The womenfolk have been talking. Told me about it earlier. They have a plan that needs a lot of prayer."

"Miss Audra? She doesn't care much for me."

Jed shrugged. "Maybe not, but she sees the truth about Christopher."

"Well, I don't want her hurt."

Jed chuckled. "That was quick. Anything else on your mind about Audra?"

Caleb set his jaw. He'd listen to them tonight, but hearing them out didn't mean he'd do what they suggested. Not one more person was going to risk their life on account of him.

❧

Naomi went to special trouble for dinner. She'd simmered a side of beef all day in onions, herbs, and greens. The biscuits looked lighter than foam off a fast-moving stream, and she'd made a rich bread pudding topped with wild strawberries. All the trouble made Audra wonder if tonight's dinner had been planned for a while. Considering what Caleb intended to do the following day and Jed's need to talk him out of it, Naomi must be doing her share.

What about me? I believe God wants me to help, but deceiving Christopher into believing I still want to marry him isn't right either. Even carefully rewording an apology sounded wrong.

I need Your guidance, God. I'm more bewildered than I can ever remember.

As soon as Naomi and Audra made the trek from the bunkhouse to feed the ranch hands, Jed and Caleb strode in. Immediately, Audra noticed a difference in the younger man. He carried himself differently, seemed self-assured. His shoulders looked a bit broader, and his voice sounded a little deeper. She wondered why, when his life was more in danger than ever before.

"You feeling all right, Miss Audra?" Jed asked. "You're a bit flushed."

Oh my, what is wrong with me? "I'm fine. Must be the cook fire. Evenin', Caleb."

"Evenin', Miss Audra."

Naomi laughed. Audra refused to look at Caleb.

"Let's eat," Naomi said a few moments later.

The four gathered around the table, and Audra ended up next to Caleb. Her unexplainable feelings toward him unnerved her. Her stomach fluttered. Perhaps she was ill.

The tantalizing smells made her stomach growl. Strange how one could lose her appetite and be hungry at the same time. Normally conversation flew in every direction, but tonight no one contributed to a single topic. Once the bread pudding disappeared and hot coffee was poured, Jed cleared his throat.

"We need to figure out what to do about Caleb's predicament, and I believe the best way to begin is with prayer." He lowered his head. "Heavenly Father, we have a heap of trouble here. You've heard me talk about the Windsor brothers before, and I know You can clear Caleb's name and stop Christopher. So now we're asking You to show us the way. Naomi and Audra have an idea, but we need to know if it is fittin' to Your plan. Show us the truth, Mighty God. In Your Son's name, amen."

Audra lifted her gaze to the people seated near her. In such a short time, she'd grown to love Jed and Naomi. And Caleb. . . He was rather peculiar, but she guessed she liked him in a brotherly way.

She took a deep breath. Then another. What did God purpose for her to do? Had she been hearing Him right this afternoon? Going against the Creator of the universe left her cold and empty.

"Caleb, like I said earlier, Naomi and Audra have devised a way to end all this," Jed said.

"Audra should tell it," Naomi said. "She's the one most involved."

Audra sensed Caleb's attention on her. Her palms suddenly grew damp. "I suppose if this is against God's will and I upset Him, He's going to let me know. This afternoon I realized Christopher is wrong and must be brought to justice."

"What are you thinking?" Caleb frowned. "If you're planning to do something dangerous, I won't have it."

"What I'm proposing is to deceive Christopher and find the evidence needed to convict him of his crimes."

Caleb stared at her sternly. "You best be telling me real fast, 'cause I suspect trouble."

Lord, show me the right path. "I'll go see Christopher tomorrow and tell him I've reconsidered the situation between us. I've been terribly upset over the robbery and shooting and can't seem to think clearly. That part's true. If he will accept my apology, I'll offer to move into the boardinghouse. I'll tell him by living in Earnest, I won't see you again, and he and I can spend more time together."

"Miss Audra, you know how he can be. . ."

"Persistent?"

"Yes—and a multitude of other things, too. What will you do about that, carry a pistol inside your apron pocket?" Caleb asked.

Jed chuckled, but Naomi hushed him.

Audra stiffened in the chair. "I am smart enough not to get myself into those kinds of situations. I plan to win him over by talking of marriage—even setting a date. I can earn his trust."

Caleb rubbed his shoulder and neck muscles. "This is

beginning to make sense, but I'm not sure it's safe. Go on and let me hear the rest of it."

"Very simple. Since he's gotten away with so many crimes, I imagine he's rather full of himself." She paused and stared at Caleb directly. "I can prod him for information while making him think he's smart. I can also express my pity for the horrible circumstances about his outlaw brother."

"And if that doesn't work?" Caleb asked.

"I'll wait until he's gone and search through his things at the parsonage and church."

Caleb's chair scraped across the floor, and he stood. "Whoa, Miss Audra. Now you're stepping into territory that could get you hurt."

"I hadn't heard this part of it either," Jed said. He glanced at Naomi.

"Neither have I," the older woman said. "Sit down, Caleb, and this time I agree with you. Christopher has killed once, and it'll be easier the next time."

The old inclination for adventure wrapped around Audra's spirit. All her life she'd settled for a boring existence while yearning to be a pioneer—a woman of strength and courage.

"I can't agree to any of this unless you promise not to set foot near the parsonage with the idea of searching it." Caleb leaned into the table. "I want to send you home to your folks in one piece, not in a pine box."

"Bravo," Naomi said.

Audra appreciated her friends' interest in her safety. "I understand what you're saying. If a situation frightens me, I'll step back."

"Miss Audra, I don't know why you're trying to help me, but I am grateful. Rest assured, I will be looking out for you. I have my ways."

Audra stared into Caleb's eyes, midnight blue. For the first time she saw something that really did frighten her.

nine

Audra walked with Jed to the parsonage. No longer did she fear her actions were wrong. Rahab had protected the Israelite spies, and the Bible listed her among the righteous. And early Christians hid Paul from those who sought to harm him. Not that she considered herself noteworthy, but the biblical examples gave her courage to help stop Christopher's unscrupulous ways.

"You're mighty quiet," Jed said. "If you're having second thoughts, I'll be glad to drive you back."

"Not at all. I was thinking about the mysteries of God. I know I'm doing the right thing, although there are folks who'll think otherwise."

"Little lady, if you believe God is guiding your path, then I wouldn't worry about what others think."

Audra smiled and linked her arm into his. "You and my papa are quite a bit alike."

Jed quickened his stride. "He asked me to watch out for you, and that's exactly what I'm doing, although he might question my judgment on this one. I'm wondering if I shouldn't whirl you around and take you back to the ranch."

"And leave Caleb to fend alone?"

He expelled a heavy sigh and said nothing.

They strolled past the church and on toward the parsonage. Her rehearsed lines set upon her lips as well as the forced smile intended for Christopher. Her stomach knotted as a grim reminder of what lay ahead, but an even greater surge reminded her of Christopher's unlawful ways. Naomi, Jed, and Caleb believed she merely planned to prod him for information. Let them believe what they wanted; she had a purpose.

A mockingbird perched on the white picket fence in front

of the parsonage. It offered a shrill call. Jed laughed. "Sorta fittin', don't you think?"

"Sure hope that bird is not making fun of us."

She climbed the steps and noted the fresh whitewash and a comfortable rocker. Clean. Homey. A calico cat curled up on a braid rug pulled to its haunches and stretched. Jed bent to stroke the animal, but it hissed and scratched at him.

Taking a deep breath, Audra knocked on the door.

"It's not too late to change your mind," Jed said barely above a whisper.

"No, sir. I'm—"

The door opened. Christopher's shoulders spanned the doorway. His wide grin radiated charm, and the surprise in his eyes was worth the anticipation.

"Audra, Jed, how good of you to stop by." He stepped back from the doorway and gestured a path to the inside. "I needed a break from preparing this week's sermon."

"I certainly don't want to keep you from God's work." Audra offered a shaky smile and gazed into his eyes. "Jed was so good to escort me here, but my purpose is to have a word with you in private."

Christopher nodded. In addition to the surprise, he tilted his head in obvious curiosity. "Would you like to walk over to the church after I pour Jed a cup of coffee?"

"Water's fine," Jed said. "I know Miss Audra's anxious to talk to you."

Christopher nodded in her direction as though immensely pleased with something. Why did a man so handsome have to be so wicked?

"Then let's not keep the lady waiting," Christopher said.

Audra chose not to speak until they reached the church. She wanted him to think she searched for the right words, which held a lot of truth. She'd been confident while talking to Jed, Naomi, and Caleb, but now she felt incredibly alone.

Me and my adventure. Who was she doing this for? The widow and her fatherless daughters? Jed and Naomi? In revenge for Papa's beating? Her grandmother's brooch? Certainly not Caleb. The man did not appeal to her. He'd gotten himself into a lot of trouble by allowing his brother to bully him. She wanted a man of strength. Audra mentally dismissed the troublesome thoughts and turned her attention to Christopher.

"Audra, I was not expecting to see you again. After our last conversation, I assumed our friendship was over." He opened the church door. "Not that I blame you after my irresponsible behavior."

"I've been thinking about what happened."

"I imagine I've become a nightmare." He shook his head. "Are you heading back to Nebraska?"

She smiled and squeezed a tear from her eye. "I hope not, which is why I'm here." She glanced at the floor—spotless, not one speck of dust. "When I think back on our conversation at Jed and Naomi's, I must admit I'm at fault, too."

His eyes softened. "However, sweet Audra? I remember it all quite clearly."

"But I insisted on the ride. Being alone for such a long time invited impropriety. Then your brother upset both of us."

He pressed his lips together. "Yes, when Caleb accused me of treating you badly, I forgot I was a man of God. He angers me so, but his wicked ways are no excuse for my own sin."

She forced another tear. "Pardon my boldness, but if I moved into the boardinghouse we wouldn't have to concern ourselves with Caleb." She shrugged. "I mean the sheriff will find him soon and bring justice to the people of Earnest, but he doesn't have to ruin our relationship." She again stared down at the wooden floor and studied an ant racing across a plank.

"You would do this for me?" Honey oozed from his words.

"I would indeed," she whispered. "I know you're a busy man with working night and day for the Lord, but perhaps I could help with some of your duties—maybe the ladies' meetings or choir."

"You are such a blessing." Christopher reached to touch her but drew back.

I am not as naïve as you think. "I want to begin again," she said. "If you think our friendship can be mended."

"I'd like nothing better." He walked down the aisle, his hands behind his back. A moment later he turned as though he were a military officer about to address his troops. "I will prove my worthiness, Audra. Things will be different, better, and we may find marriage in our future after all."

"I believe we shall." She walked toward him. When they stood within inches of each other, she stood on tiptoe and planted a light kiss on his cheek. "I will do my best to be understanding of the way you must deal with Caleb."

"What have I done to deserve such a godly woman?"

"I believe I am the lucky one. Your father sent me here to possibly help you in your ministry, and I desire to do all I can to fulfill my obligations."

Perhaps she'd gone too far.

⁊⁊

Caleb lifted the post-hole digger then thrust it into the ground. Sweat streamed down his face and soaked his bandanna. He'd worked since sunup setting fence posts for Jed. Not that he didn't want to help his friend, but he'd rather be working his own place. His foreman was a loyal man, and the sheriff knew it. The law had deputies planted on every corner of his ranch looking for Caleb Windsor. No point in putting any of his hands in danger. Or in jail.

He peered up and shielded his eyes from the westward slant of the sun. No wonder his stomach growled. Naomi had packed him biscuits and bacon, but he hadn't taken the time to stop for a noonday meal. Frustration pushed him on. First Jed and Naomi had gotten themselves knee-deep in protecting him. Now Audra was involved. She didn't have the Masterses' grit—and a mistake could get her killed. If she hadn't looked up at him with those light blue eyes framed by all that blonde hair, then poured pure sugar into every word, he never would have agreed. The truth be known, if Audra had handed him a noose, he'd have tied it around his neck.

Smitten, Jed called it. A plumb fool is what Caleb called it. She'd hit him blind side and knocked out all his good sense. The truth hammered at his heart: Miss Audra still looked at him as though he were an outlaw. He sank the post-hole digger into the moist earth and deliberated the whole thing again. Even if he declared his devotion to her, what did he have to offer but a life on the run? He blew out a heavy sigh and watched his sweat drop into the hole.

The situation with his brother had to change soon, or Caleb would need to leave the country. Jed had been right about the sheriff not believing Chris's old gang member. Caleb knew it, too; he simply wanted an easy solution. *Lord, forgive me for putting good people in danger.*

In the distance a rider approached. He dropped the post-hole digger and headed toward his rifle leaning against an oak tree. He whistled for his horse. Leaving Jed's tools, he swung onto the saddle and headed for the trees. Once he found safety in the thick growth, he watched the rider approach.

Caleb studied the rider, an older man and a stranger to the territory. His beard looked unkempt, and his clothes showed the marks of days in the saddle. The man dismounted and studied the area where Caleb had been working. A moment later, he bent and examined the boot prints. *He knows those are fresh tracks. Lawman, maybe a bounty hunter.* The man stood and walked a few paces in Caleb's direction. He tipped his hat toward the trail. *He thinks I'm stupid. Mister, I have learned a trick or two in my life.*

While the stranger made his way back to his mount, Caleb nudged his horse's flanks. He knew every place to hide within miles. Somehow he had to get word to Jed; Chris could have set a trap and included the Masterses in it. Troubles kept piling up, reminding Caleb of drifting snow in a mountain pass.

Two hours later, Caleb felt certain he'd shaken the stranger. Hidden behind a rock on a lofty peak, he watched the man circle around, check Caleb's trail, and head off in the opposite direction.

That could be a trap, too.

Lord, I sure could use a little help here. Would You blind my trail to that man for good?

He waited awhile longer, half expecting the stranger to reappear. Caleb led his horse around to the other side of the peak and studied the outline of the horizon. He looked for the man to come riding into view. Shadows crested the area around him and, unless the man could see after dark, Caleb was safe. *Thank You.*

Best he head to Jed and Naomi's and see if they'd heard about anything peculiar.

He rode the last few miles to the Masterses' ranch concealed by a cloak of darkness. Good thing he knew the way. Doubts plagued him about the stranger—hard to predict what a desperate man might do, and both the sheriff and Chris were anxious to get rid of him. He hid his horse in a grove of trees behind the corral and waited until he knew the hands were inside the bunkhouse. He stole around the barn to the house, blending with the forces of the night. Fortunately the dogs knew him, or he'd be in trouble. A light shone through the kitchen window. Everything looked normal, but still he waited. Then he caught sight of the stranger drinking coffee with Jed and Naomi. A Winchester lay across his lap. That didn't look like a sociable conversation to Caleb, especially when the man's dirty finger rested on the trigger. He crept to an open window and bent to listen.

"I've been told you folks could tell me where to find Caleb Windsor."

"Reckon you got yourself some bad information," Jed said. "Try talking to the sheriff."

"The sheriff sent me. Said the preacher's woman told him you were hiding Caleb Windsor."

Would Audra have done that? Caleb refused to believe she was capable of such treachery, but he'd misjudged Chris all his life. To consider his brother and Audra working together against him sent an explosion of rage through his body.

"You mean Miss Audra?" Jed asked, not an ounce of surprise in his words.

"Didn't hear her name, but I saw her. Yellow hair, pretty, and from Nebrasky."

"Mercy," Naomi said. "I have no idea where she would have gotten that information."

"Sheriff said she came to him last week with the news. He wired for me."

"Last week?" Jed asked.

"I recollect the telegram said Tuesday mornin'."

Audra was here then. She didn't leave until Wednesday.

"And who are you?" Jed asked.

"Jim Hawk. I'm a bounty hunter."

Smell like one, too. No wonder you tracked me like a mountain cat.

A chair scooted across the wooden floor. "Mr. Hawk, my wife and I don't know anything about what you're talking about, so you best be on your way."

"I plan on staying a spell until Windsor shows up."

Naomi laughed. "You'll be here until the next frost. Want some more coffee?"

"Don't mind if I do. Think I'll take it with me while your husband and me take a look at the barns and bunkhouse."

"And if I refuse?" Jed asked.

"Then I'll have to shoot you in the name of the law."

"Is that what the sheriff told you?"

"He didn't say one way or the other. It's how I take care of business."

Caleb had heard enough. Between the sound of Hawk's orders and Naomi telling Jed to do what the man said, Caleb put together a plan.

Hawk and Jed headed toward the bunkhouse. Caleb understood the bounty hunter would pump lead into any of them who objected to his search.

"Here I am." Caleb stepped into the path of the two men. He held his rifle behind him for fear the light from the kitchen and bunkhouse might reveal it. "You want me for something?"

Hawk chuckled. "Looks like that gal was right." He lifted his Winchester. "You're going with me."

Caleb lifted his rifle. "I don't think so." Even in the night air, the man smelled like he never bathed.

Jed spun in Hawk's direction and knocked the Winchester from his hand. In the next breath Jed snatched it up. Caleb stepped in and shoved his rifle under Hawk's chin. "Now, you and I are going to talk. I have a heap of questions."

"And if I refuse?"

"You won't." Caleb pointed toward the barn. "That looks like a good place. How about joining us, Jed?" He needed his friend with him.

"Sure."

The three moved inside the barn where Jed lit a lantern.

"Sit down." Caleb pushed Hawk to the floor. He had to find out who sent him. If he let Hawk go, the man would kill him "Who are you working for?"

"The sheriff. I'm a bounty hunter."

"I know the sheriff." Jed held up the lantern. "And he wouldn't hire a two-bit bounty hunter to do a lawman's job."

"You forget the gal told him where to find you."

"Audra Lenders was here last Tuesday," Jed said. "She's been living with us until two days ago."

"So that means Chris Windsor hired you," Caleb said.

"I said I'm a bounty hunter. The sheriff wired me last week just like I told you."

Realization nearly strangled him. The sheriff and Chris were working together.

ten

Five days later, Audra felt the pangs of regret regarding her move into the boardinghouse. Loneliness cast its shroud around her, with Christopher as her only companion. Three women from his church had paid enjoyable visits, but Christopher said they were gossips and not to establish a friendship with them. They hadn't appeared to be busybodies at all, but she expected him to isolate her from the community. Her aloofness would feed into his cause when she attempted to expose him.

She missed Naomi and Jed almost as much as she missed Mama and Papa. Christopher left her at times to call on his congregation, or so he claimed. Her thoughts lingered on which was worse—enduring his company or being alone. She read and took walks, but rain had forced her inside.

When Audra considered her past anger toward Caleb, she faced a truth about herself. His good qualities were what she wanted in Christopher. Maybe some of the anger pointed at her, too. She had her hopes built on being a pastor's wife, and that aspect propelled her into a fairy-tale world. Being deceived by a man who professed to be a leader of God's people didn't help either.

What surprised Audra the most was how she longed for Caleb. In the beginning, she believed the two men looked identical, but their disposition and spiritual commitments distinguished their physical appearance. Every time they'd talked, he'd been a gentleman. He'd come to her rescue and put himself in danger. Caleb treated her like a fragile porcelain doll. He didn't impose his will or push her toward conducting herself in an ungodly manner. More and more she realized how much she had misjudged him.

She did care for him, very much.

Despair paralyzed her emotions. She wanted to see Jed and Naomi and possibly catch a glimpse of Caleb. Determination seized her the following morning when she shared breakfast with Christopher.

"Would you take me to Jed and Naomi's early tomorrow morning?" she asked.

He cut a generous slice of ham. "Do you think it's wise with my brother still roaming the countryside?

"If I'm visiting Jed and Naomi, then neither you nor I have a reason to worry."

He lifted his gaze to reach hers then smiled. "I do have some calls to make near the Masterses' ranch. I could tend to them and pick you up before supper."

"Perfect." She hadn't thought he'd agree so quickly, and for his concession she was grateful. "Can we leave before sunup?"

"Why? Has my company bored you?"

She touched his arm and forced a smile. "Not at all, Christopher. Jed and Naomi are like my parents, and you have to admit I haven't made any friends here in Earnest."

He lifted a brow, and she saw the look in his eyes—the same stomach-grinding sneer he gave Papa just before he hit him. At that moment, Audra despised him, more so than at any other time. How long before he unleashed his temper like a caged animal? "Audra, it isn't my fault you are unsociable. There are many good women in the church."

Whom you won't let me near. She didn't dare rile him and lose her opportunity to see Jed and Naomi, or worse yet fail to catch Christopher breaking the law.

"I'm sorry. The ladies who came to see me were pleasant, but you didn't think they were suitable companions for me."

He nodded slowly. "I will look into the matter today. I have a few women in mind who would be good for you." Suddenly his demeanor changed. He reached for her hand. "I don't want my sweet Audra lonely or bored. I'll escort you to the Masterses before sunrise in the morning. I must keep my lady from pining away for Nebraska and womenfolk company."

"Thank you." She kept her tone low and respectful to keep from screaming at him. She understood exactly what he was doing: catering to her until she set a wedding date. His charm may speak for him to the rest of this town, but she'd seen his other side.

The following morning, Christopher drove Audra to the Masterses' ranch.

"I really appreciate this," she said, "and your offer to introduce me to appropriate women. I trust your judgment completely when it comes to guiding me, especially if we are to marry." The thought churned her stomach.

"You honor me, dear Audra. I apologize for the way I spoke to you yesterday morning. It's my fault that you haven't met the proper women of this town. Yesterday I went by the homes of some of our finest families and made introductions for you."

"Thank you. I guess I wanted too much too soon."

"Nonsense. We've waited all our lives to find each other. And we are eager to have a home and fine friends to go with it."

"You understand me very well," Audra said. All the while she'd rather confront him about his outlaw activities. God have mercy on him for killing a man while hiding behind the deception of a pastor.

❧

"Mercy, Audra, seems like you've been gone forever." Naomi drew her into a hug. "I hope you two are staying for a while."

"I'm leaving to make some calls," Christopher said. "But Audra wants to spend the day."

"If you don't mind," Audra said. "I'll help with whatever you need. This is Tuesday, a baking day like Thursday, as I recall."

"And we will have a splendid time." Naomi smiled. Her round eyes crinkled, reminding Audra of an old Indian woman who lived in Nebraska.

"Then I will leave you ladies to your fun." Christopher tipped his hat to both of them. "I may need to pray for Jed today."

Audra forced a laugh, so glad to be rid of him. "I will see you near evening."

"For supper," Naomi said.

"Thank you, ma'am. I don't want to impose, but your cooking is far superior to the boardinghouse's. I'll look forward to it."

Audra watched him drive the wagon down the road. As soon as he ventured beyond earshot, relief swept over her. "Oh, Naomi, he makes me ill."

The woman wrapped her arm around Audra's waist as they strolled toward the house. "We have much to talk about while making bread."

"But I have so little to tell you." Sadness laced Audra's words. "I so wanted to have something important."

"It's only been a few days. These things take time." She sighed. "I know you haven't had breakfast, so let's talk after that." She hesitated. "I have a few things to tell you."

Audra would rather have waited on breakfast and talked first, but she respected her friend's wishes.

After breakfast, Naomi pushed aside her coffee cup. "We had a visitor a few days ago, a bounty hunter by the name of Jim Hawk." Lines deepened in Naomi's face.

Audra listened. This didn't sound good at all.

"He said Sheriff Reynolds hired him to find Caleb hiding out at our ranch. He also said you told the sheriff about Caleb being here."

Audra's eyes widened. "I never did such a thing."

Naomi shook her head. "We know you didn't. I think Jed, Caleb, and I are better judges of character than that. But Hawk claimed you went to the sheriff last Tuesday."

"I was here." Audra's pulse quickened. Realization caused her to shiver. "Then Sheriff Reynolds and Christopher are working together."

"We believe so."

Audra stood and carried her coffee mug out to the front porch. Her mind spun with the hopelessness of helping Caleb. No one would ever believe his innocence with the pastor and the sheriff on the wrong side of the law. How did Satan gather such a foothold in Earnest?

"But we have God on our side," she said.

"And He is all we need," Naomi said behind her. "I admit this is my biggest test of faith. Jed and I have been through a lot together, but trusting God to deliver Caleb is hard, real hard."

Audra nodded. She kept her back turned to hide her tears. A month ago she didn't know Jed, Naomi, Caleb, or Christopher. Her future looked optimistic, and the idea of an adventure in Colorado was filled with romantic notions. Now all the beauty had been marred by evil men. Who else could be involved? "I'm afraid—for you, Jed, and Caleb. I thought once we found the evidence to prove Christopher's guilt, we could go to Sheriff Reynolds. So what is the answer?"

"Prayer. We simply need to pray for guidance," Naomi said. "When we join Jed at noon, we must have a prayer meetin'. He's checking on new calves."

Audra blinked and swiped at the tears glazing her cheeks. She faced Naomi with a trembling smile. "I'm ready to make bread."

"And we'll talk and pray."

Once the bread dough rested in wooden bowls, left covered to rise, Naomi and Audra weeded the vegetable garden with its sprouts of lettuce, tomatoes, onions, and green beans. Audra worked with a vengeance.

"Are those weeds Christopher and the sheriff?" Naomi asked.

Audra glanced up and then took a look at how deep she'd plunged the hoe into the earth. She laughed for the first time since she'd learned about Jim Hawk's accusation.

Naomi laughed with her.

"I guess those two had better stay clear of my temper," Audra said.

"You could run all three of those rascals out of Colorado all by yourself."

The laughter continued and eased the anger and depression threatening to overtake her. *God is the judge of Christopher and the sheriff, not me. An ill temperament doesn't solve a thing.*

"Looks like I can fry up a chicken to take to Jed." Naomi dabbed the perspiration from her face with her apron. "I had no idea this weeding would go so fast."

"Go ahead, and I'll finish here," Audra said. "I still have some ugliness in me that needs to be dealt with."

While she finished hoeing, her thoughts wandered to Caleb. She'd like to see him, talk to him if possible.

"Where are your dreams?" Naomi asked. She held out a cup of water. "I've been talking to you for the past few minutes, and you were far from here.

Startled, Audra took the water. "I'm sorry."

"You're blushing. Maybe I should have asked who was on your mind."

Audra lifted the hoe and glanced over the garden. "Looks like the weeds have headed for someone else's garden, because they are gone from here."

"You're ignoring me." Naomi wagged her finger. "So your thoughts are softening toward Caleb?"

Audra nodded slowly. "How is he?"

"Quiet. Rather sad. This business between him and Christopher has always been difficult, but I think other things are bothering him, too."

Her heart quickened. "Christopher said the sheriff plans to sell Caleb's ranch to pay back some of the money he's stolen."

"We'll see him at noon," Naomi said. "He's giving Jed a hand."

Audra's gaze flew to her friend's face. She dare not utter another word. Caleb had enough problems without adding a woman to them. In a few hours she'd see him. She'd learned some things since living at the boardinghouse. Nothing grand, but at least she wasn't sitting idle.

Soon the noon meal sat in the back of the wagon, and the two women left the ranch. The thought of seeing Caleb made her feel like a skittish cat. She kept telling herself to calm down, but it didn't help.

"Should I have given you a dose of castor oil?" Naomi chuckled.

"Castor oil?"

"At least you'd have something else to think about. Calm yourself, dear. I see Jed and Caleb heading our way."

Audra studied the figures of the two men riding toward them. Caleb sat straight in the saddle. *Don't stare at him. Look at Jed. Remember what you need to tell both of them.*

Naomi should have given her the castor oil.

❧

Caleb guessed Audra rode beside Naomi. He searched in every direction to make sure his brother didn't accompany them. Did she ride to the ranch alone? Had something happened? Was she in danger? He attempted to settle his anxious heart. She'd been in his waking and sleeping moments for days—a vision of grace and loveliness. He stumbled over what to say. Best he simply be polite and let her speak her mind.

"Is this our Audra?" Jed asked. "I don't want a thing to eat. All I need is to feast my eyes on her pretty face."

"Jed Masters, you're a married man." Naomi shook her finger at him.

Audra laughed and blushed with Jed's compliment. "It's wonderful to see you—both of you."

She appeared to snatch a glimpse of Caleb, and her cheeks reddened a little more.

Jed dismounted and helped his wife down from the wagon. Caleb held his breath and realized he needed to do the same. The moment his hands touched Audra's slender waist, he felt her tremble. Did he do something wrong? She must be afraid of him.

"Thank you," she whispered. He stole a look at her face. No longer did he see the doubt and distrust from the past. In their place rested another emotion, one he didn't know how to interpret.

"Have you learned anything more about Chris?" Jed asked.

"Naomi told me a horrible story about him and Sheriff Reynolds. But what I have to report is small. I'm sorry."

"You've been in town for only a few days, and I apologize for asking," Jed said. "Let's eat first, and then we can talk."

"And pray," Naomi added.

Jed asked the blessing and for guidance about the hardships facing Caleb. "Help us to forgive those who intend us harm," he said. "Watch over our Audra, and keep her safe. And, Lord, we can't do a thing about this unless You fight the battle for us."

They ate on the soft grass with the food placed on an old quilt. They talked as though they hadn't seen each other for weeks. No one mentioned Chris or the sheriff. Caleb forced himself to eat Naomi's fried chicken, pinto beans, and hot bread. He loved her cooking and he was hungry, but today his mind wrestled with other things. If he failed to eat with his normal appetite, they all could tell something was wrong.

His heart had been captured by one young woman with sun-colored hair and pale blue eyes, and he couldn't do a thing about it.

"I want to tell you what I've learned." Audra's voice rang like sweet music through his spirit. "It's not as much as I'd like, but it's a beginning."

"I'm wondering again if this isn't too dangerous," Caleb said.

"Too late. I've already made a few plans of my own," Audra said. "As soon as he leaves town, I'm determined to find the evidence we need. Jed is allowing me to take one of his mares back to Earnest."

Jed cleared his throat. "The horse is in case you need to leave town."

"I don't like the idea of you ever needing a horse. Besides, what are we going to do with evidence once we have it?" Caleb asked. "No one in town will believe us."

Jed waved his hand. "When we get the evidence, we could make a trip to the governor's office." He rubbed his chin. "Work's caught up here. Think I'll head to Denver and see what I can learn."

"What makes you think Governor Eaton would listen without proof?"

"Because our story is so outlandish he may believe it's true."

Caleb shrugged. "Possibly." He turned to Audra. "What have you learned?"

"That he's quickly losing patience with me. I refuse to be alone with him, and he wants to marry badly. I have to work fast, or I'm going to be wed." She laughed, but he could hear the trepidation in her voice. "He's finding it harder and harder to play the role of a pastor in my presence."

I'm afraid for you. This idea is foolishness. They needed proof, a place where Chris hid the money and the other stolen items—but not at the risk of Audra's safety. "Anything else?" Caleb asked.

"One day he had a call to make to the widow of the man who was killed in the stagecoach robbery. When he returned, I questioned him about Belle's welfare and her little girls, and he repeated their conversation. The next day I saw her walking to the cemetery. I joined Belle and asked if Pastor Windsor's visit the day before had been helpful. She said I must have been mistaken, because the pastor hadn't visited since the funeral." Audra peered into Caleb's face as though determined to find the evidence they needed. "The next time he speaks of making a call, I'll follow him."

eleven

Audra silently challenged Caleb to argue with her. The longer she spent time with him, the more she realized her feelings were not a passing fancy, but the kind of love seen in Mama and Papa and her married brothers and sisters. Caleb most likely despised her for some of the accusations she'd spit his way in the beginning, and she couldn't blame him. After all, she'd been convinced he was an outlaw.

"You will not put yourself in danger," Caleb said.

Each of his words shook her will like Papa swinging an axe over a stack of wood. "I most certainly will. Have you forgotten the sheriff is in this? And the bounty hunter and whoever else is after the reward?"

"I'll hang before I risk you being dragged into the middle of this." Not a muscle moved on his face.

"I'm already in the middle. That happened when your brother stopped the stage and I witnessed a murder." Irritation gave her an edge of courage.

"This is my problem."

"And you are the most stubborn man I've ever met."

"Arguing won't solve a thing," Jed said with a wave of a drumstick. "If there's anyone close by looking for Caleb, you two will have them down on us in no time."

Calm down. "I apologize," Audra said. "I'm a little angry."

"So am I," Caleb said.

Naomi stood and walked to the wagon. "I have a few slices of milk cake here. It might sweeten Audra and Caleb's disposition." She brought the cake to the quilt.

"I know it's delicious, but I'm quite full." Audra sensed the mounting warmth reaching her neck and face and realized her friends could see her discomfort.

"I've had more than enough," Caleb said. "If I stuff one more bite into this body, I'll not be able to do a lick of work."

Jed handed his plate to Naomi. "Pile it high, wife. Know what I think?"

Audra glanced his way, not sure if she wanted to hear Jed's remark to his wife.

"Not sure, tell me," Naomi said.

"I think these two bickering young people should take a walk and settle whatever's ailing them."

"I agree." Naomi sliced a generous piece of the cake for Jed and then herself. "I can't seem to figure out what's wrong with those two. Any idea, Jed?"

He swallowed a mouthful. "Yep, I do. It's—"

"Let's go, Audra." Caleb set his plate on the quilt.

Her heart fluttered against her chest like a hummingbird's wings. *Please, Jed. I'll be humiliated.* "I'm ready, as long as Naomi will wait until we get back to gather up the food."

"Get on out of here. Jed and I have things to discuss." Naomi waved them away like she was scattering feed to chickens.

Audra hurriedly joined Caleb before the Masterses spoke another word. They walked down a green hill toward a winding stream. As they ventured closer, the sound of the gurgling stream and the sight of little whitecaps offered the peace she desperately craved.

"What are we supposed to discuss?" Caleb's tone conveyed his frustration.

"Our bickering."

"Well, we wouldn't be fussing if you'd listen to reason."

"Me?" She raised a brow. "I'm trying to help you—keep you from getting killed."

"And I'm doing the same thing for you."

"Lower your voice or the whole state will hear you."

Caleb inhaled then exhaled. "I simply want to make sure you're safe. We both know Chris can't be trusted."

Audra's irritation seeped through to the surface. "Jed and

Naomi have been in danger for quite awhile. I don't hear you voicing concern about them."

"Jed and Naomi are different." His attention focused on a hawk soaring overhead. He shielded his eyes against the sun and followed the grand bird's flight.

She watched the hawk, too, but her thoughts were on Caleb's insinuation. "How are they different? Are you saying I'm not smart enough to help?"

He whirled around to face her. "Where did you come up with such a stupid idea?"

"There, you said it. You think I'm stupid." She'd been right all along. How could she possibly care for a man who made her this angry?

"I never even thought such a thing." Caleb's eyes flashed.

"Good. Because I don't intend to sit back and read or knit or write long letters to my family in Nebraska while Christopher continues to break the law." She caught herself before saying another word. "I made a commitment to do whatever is necessary to stop your brother. Mercy, Caleb, just because I'm a woman doesn't mean I haven't any sense."

"I told you I didn't say or mean anything of the like."

She crossed her arms. "We are supposed to be settling our differences."

"That's impossible."

"And I agree."

"We could call a truce. That would make Jed and Naomi happy."

Despite her aggravation, she laughed. "All right. Let's walk a bit."

They strolled on, neither saying a word. She searched for a question or comment beyond the topic of lawbreakers. "Tell me about your boyhood."

He shrugged. "Chris and I did everything together. Mostly got into trouble." He paused. "We lived in western Nebraska not far from the Platte River. We loved the river, fishing, swimming—as long as it was wet."

"I'm glad you got along well."

"We did." He sighed and gazed out to the snow-capped mountains. "When I think about how we were then, I see why Chris is so selfish."

"You don't have to talk about this."

"I don't mind. It's my fault. Whatever he wanted to do, I agreed. I looked out for him, protected him. I remember one time when we were thirteen. We'd been playing near the river, trying to catch a mess of fish. The river was swollen, and he fell in. Chris got caught up in the current. Scared me to death. I jumped in and pulled him out. We both near drowned."

Looked like Caleb had always jumped in to save his brother. "You saved his life." Admiration laced her thoughts.

"I guess. Later he asked me why, and I said because we were brothers. I loved him. Chris shook his head and studied me for the longest time before he spoke. He said he didn't know if he would have saved me. He'd been too scared."

Startled, Audra peered up into his face. "What did you say?"

Caleb smiled, but she could tell he hid his sadness. "I told him not to worry. I'd always be there to help him." He chuckled. "And I've been doing it ever since."

Audra thought about the story. Caleb's recollection painted a clear picture of how two people chose two different paths.

"What about you?" he asked. "Brothers and sisters?"

Audra wasn't certain she wanted to talk about herself, especially with her mind focused on two young boys who were incredibly different. "Nothing interesting to tell. I'm the youngest of eight—stubborn, spoiled—and neither Papa nor Mama wanted to let me go."

He smiled. "I've seen your stubborn streak, but that's not bad."

"Should I remind you why we're taking this walk?" She stifled a giggle.

"We called a truce, remember?"

His tone left an unsettling sensation in the pit of her stomach. "But I haven't changed my mind about what I want to do to bring your brother to justice."

"But you will."

Those words washed over her like ice water. "I think not, sir." She whirled around and started up the hill without him.

"Audra."

She stopped but kept her attention straight ahead.

"Why are you determined to help me?"

Clenching her fists, she considered the question. A myriad answers danced across her mind. "You already know I'm angry about Papa's treatment and the poor widow left to raise her daughters alone." *Don't force me to look at you, or my eyes will give away my feelings.*

"Such nobility you have, Audra."

"Thank you." She started walking again and left him far behind. Justice was a noble cause, but the hint of love tore at her sensibilities. Up ahead she saw a man standing by the Masterses' wagon. Fear squeezed her heart, for Christopher had his back to her. Where had he left his wagon unless he hid it from view?

She bent and hurried back down the hill, nearly slipping in the process. Caleb must be warned. Christopher could have men combing the area. Trailing up the path, Caleb stared at the ground, obviously unaware of her descent. She waved her hands at him. *Please don't shout at me.* In the next instant, he looked up. She touched her forefinger to her lips and rushed to him.

"Your brother is with Naomi and Jed," she said. "I neither saw his wagon nor whether others were with him."

He nodded and took her hand. "Let's cross the stream and get out of sight."

She lifted her skirt with one hand and took his hand with the other. They stepped on round, slippery steppingstones in a shallow area, where she nearly fell into the cold water. He steadied her, and she caught her breath. In the next instant, they disappeared under a canopy of trees. Conscious of the strong hand gripping hers, Audra realized, as she had before, that a life with Caleb would be spent on the run. It really wouldn't be a life at all but a flight from one safe haven to another.

"I think if you pick a few wildflowers and head back to the wagon, Chris might not suspect the truth," he said once they were into the depths of the trees.

"He could count the plates from lunch."

"I imagine Naomi has cleaned up," Caleb said. "She's used to covering up for me."

"I pray so." She glanced about at the pastel watercolor array of wildflowers nodding their heads in the breeze. "I'll gather up the wildflowers." She gasped. "Your horse!"

"Out of sight in the hills."

"Praise God."

He laughed. "This is my life, Audra."

Again the realization of his perilous existence shook her. Not only would this life be a hardship for her, but her presence would also slow him—endanger him. "I'm so sorry, Caleb. I promise I will do everything in my power, with God's help, to free you from this." She swallowed her emotion.

"For the sake of those who've been wronged."

She wondered if his statement was a question, for the look in his eyes spoke of an inquiry—an inquiry of the heart.

"I mustn't tarry," she said. "Christopher will not be pleased."

He squeezed her hand lightly. "Godspeed, Audra. Please, let's not argue anymore. And promise me you will not put yourself in danger."

"I'll do my best." She broke away and snatched up the senseless wildflowers, crossed the stream, and hurried up the hill to where Christopher awaited: the most incorrigible man she'd ever known.

Already she missed the man behind her. *Caleb, I'm only a woman, but a woman who loves you.*

"Audra," Naomi called.

She lifted her gaze to the top of the hill and waved. "I'm coming."

Naomi clutched her skirts and headed downward. "Here she is, Christopher." She shook her head. "Where have you been? Oh, I see, wildflowers."

Christopher stood several feet behind her with Jed.

"I'm sorry. Every step I took there were more flowers, and then I saw these yellow ones on the other side of a stream. I nearly slipped on the rocks getting to them."

The older woman reached her and expelled a heavy sigh. "I didn't know how else to warn you," she whispered.

"I saw him earlier."

"Has my sweet lady been picking flowers?" A grin spread over Christopher's face. "You are so much like a whimsical child, and I'm fortunate to call you mine."

His words clawed at her heart, along with his endless lies and deceit. She forced a smile. "I hope you haven't been waiting long."

"Long enough to be concerned, but the Masters said you'd gone for a walk."

She laughed. "If I'd brought a pole, I might have followed the water to where I could fish for trout. And I'd be there still."

"Aren't you the youngest in your family?" he asked.

She nodded. "And used to getting my own way."

He linked her arm with his. "I don't mind. Beauty like yours needs to be indulged. You must ease this heart soon and tell me when we can marry."

She despised her role in this charade. *Dear Lord, I pray You are leading me in this, for I'm beginning to feel vile.* "I think we can decide on a date. Perhaps on the ride back to Earnest?"

Christopher shouted like an Indian heading into battle. "Did you hear that, Jed? We're deciding on a wedding day this evening."

"Make sure you give her plenty of time to sew her weddin' dress and all those other things women fuss about," Jed said.

"I agree," Naomi said. "Audra will be the prettiest bride Earnest has ever seen."

Christopher laughed. "If it will hurry the big day, I'll get all the women in town to help her."

How long must this all continue?

&

Caleb realized the time had come for him to take action and stop allowing his friends to risk their lives in protecting him. A meeting between Jed and Governor Eaton held a lot of merit, but Caleb didn't need a trip to Denver to understand the authorities required hard evidence. Audra had made headway with the widow, and maybe the woman would testify when the time came. Still, the answers always returned to the same problem: Someone needed to locate the money and stolen goods. Chris probably stored the items right under everyone's nose.

I've been a fool. Why didn't I see the sheriff and Chris were in this together? Jim Hawk may be a part of their gang, too. Who else is involved?

Chris had always been the clever one, but desperation had a way of smarting up a man, too. And Caleb had been dodging the law and his outlaw brother for a long time. Now, with the realization that a fine woman had touched his heart, he had even more reasons to bring justice to the surface.

He allowed his thoughts to linger on Audra awhile longer. If Chris wasn't arrested soon, she could get hurt. He saw a willful side of her that worried him and a fearlessness woven with determination. He also saw a spark of caring. The latter could cause her to act without thinking. He should know; all manner of reason left him when he looked into those heaven-sent eyes. The two of them didn't dare be alone again, not until Chris sat behind bars.

In the past, Caleb had eluded those after him. He played a cat-and-mouse game, and the law or his brother did the chasing. With other innocent people involved, he realized the time had come to trail Chris's every move. He'd follow his brother day and night until he found the evidence.

I'll settle for a bullet or a noose around my neck before I allow those near me to suffer.

twelve

"You cannot wander off anymore," Christopher said. Evening snatches of light played through tree branches in shadows that reminded her of giant fingers. Audra thought how romantic a wagon ride could be with the right man. She'd gladly exchange the queasiness in her stomach for a glowing light in her heart—for Caleb.

"I couldn't resist the wildflowers. You remember Nebraska. This is so different, and I wanted to capture a part of Colorado beauty."

"At the risk of my brother capturing you? Sweetheart, he could hold you for ransom—he is capable of a lot of things."

She swallowed an angry retort. She must continue playing naïve. "I'm sorry you were worried. I'm used to living free and enjoying the land."

"And you will soon again. Caleb can't run forever, unless he leaves the territory."

"I dearly wish the outlaws were caught." *And you were behind bars.*

He sighed. "I know, and so do I. In the meantime, think about the possible danger. I'm afraid my brother is up to something—and you might be part of it."

She touched her lips. "Has he said so?"

Christopher paused, most likely to conjure up a story. "He said you were much too beautiful for me. And he reminded me that he had kissed you first."

Someday everyone will know the truth. "How cruel."

"He made a few threats, but I refuse to repeat them." He shook his head and took a deep breath. "Just promise me you will take heed."

"I will. I can do no less than to ensure you peace of mind."

He glanced her way and grinned. "You can give me great joy by telling me when we can wed." He chuckled. "Tomorrow?"

Audra detested the tone in his voice, as though he might truly care. She wanted the charade to end soon. This very night if possible. She'd gladly tell him how despicable he was and never see him again, but the problems wouldn't vanish.

Her finances had dwindled to a critical stage. No matter how many times she counted her meager funds, she had barely enough to live at the boardinghouse two weeks longer. She must seek employment and accept the fact that Christopher would be furious with the idea.

"Are you going to make this poor heart beg?" he asked, interrupting her musings.

"Of course not. I think perhaps four weeks from this Sunday?"

"No sooner?"

His pitiful begging unnerved her. "Christopher, I want everything to be perfect, and even four weeks gives me little time." She considered touching his arm, but the fear of him stopping the wagon to steal a kiss halted her. "Won't you need to summon a pastor from a neighboring town?"

"We could ride there tomorrow and make arrangements."

"Is he a friend of yours? I mean is he a good pastor?"

"The best. And I want the best for us. We will remember our wedding day for the rest of our lives."

And my wedding won't be with you. "Now I feel better."

"Shall I kiss you soundly to seal the date?"

She gasped and stiffened. "I think not. I'm saving all of my affections for our wedding night."

He laughed. "Such a surprise you are, Audra. To taste your sweet lips, I'll wait the month's time. I can hardly wait to tell our congregation. They will be pleased."

And I have four weeks to find the evidence to prove you guilty of all the crimes blamed on Caleb. His kiss is the one I crave, and his arms are the ones I long to hold me.

Back in her room, Audra asked God to give her continued guidance and strength. For certain the next time Christopher made calls, she'd keep a short distance behind him.

❧

Audra dreaded Sunday. To her, announcing the wedding date to the congregation was like standing in front of God and lying. Deceiving God's people on a Sunday morning worship service? Had she stooped to the same level as Christopher? The reality made her stomach churn. She wanted to bathe in the hottest water imaginable and scrub her skin raw.

"You will make a wonderful pastor's wife," a matronly woman said. "Our sweet pastor needs someone to help him with the responsibilities of the church. It appears to me that you are as beautiful on the inside as you are on the outside."

"Thank you." Audra smiled to keep from crying. Were her near-tears a result of misleading these people or the idea of possibly disappointing God? Or both?

"We need to get you involved in Bible study and our other ladies' meetings." The same woman nodded as if to punctuate her words. "But we'll wait until after the weddin'. My husband is one of the elders, so you and I will get to spend lots of time together."

"I appreciate your thinking about me." What else could she say? It was easy to make a fuss over small children and babies, even spend a few hours in the company of godly women. But discussing her wifely duties after exchanging marital vows with Christopher? Heaven forbid!

She hated all of this. Audra took a deep breath to control her emotions. She wanted a home and family someday, but not with Christopher.

A little boy tugged on her yellow and green flowered dress. She lifted the toddler into her arms, glad for the diversion. "Where is your mama?" she asked.

He promptly stuck his thumb into his mouth and leaned on her shoulder.

"You have the touch," another woman said. "Edna Sue,

come look where your son is."

A young woman with dark hair and eyes stepped up to her. "I hope he hasn't bothered you, Miss Audra. Although when he gets tired he is picky about whom he wants to hold him." She held out her arms, and the child reached for her.

"I enjoyed your son for the brief time I held him." Audra patted his back. He closed his eyes and snuggled up to his mother.

The members thinned out from the churchyard until she stood alone. With no sign of Christopher, she climbed the steps to the church. She hoped he'd left to tend to something—anything—but he always waited for her. The cross on the wall behind the pulpit caught her attention. She hadn't considered this church a real house of God since she learned the truth about Christopher. But now, alone and surrounded by the symbols of worship, she felt the presence of the heavenly Father.

God is here, because those folks who worship seek Him with all their hearts.

She smiled and sensed the love and peace she'd come to recognize as the Lord's special gift to her. If only Christopher had listened to God's voice and responded in obedience instead of rebellion.

Glancing about, she noticed a few hymnals hadn't been replaced, a task she normally completed with Christopher. A few moments later, she had everything in order and still no sign of him.

A small room to the right caught her attention. Christopher entered the church sanctuary from this area and made his announcements before beginning the sermon. The offering plate was stored in the small room. Perhaps he and the elder who held the position as treasurer were gathering up today's offering.

Audra moved to the door and listened. Hearing nothing, she saw it wasn't closed completely and pushed it slightly with her finger, just enough to take a peek. Christopher stood counting the money from the collection plate. She started to speak since he didn't note her presence. At that moment, he stuck a handful of the money in his pocket and the rest into the bag that went to the treasurer.

Immediately she stepped back and tiptoed to a pew midway through the church. Trembling, she picked up a hymnal and pretended to read it. Her frenzied emotions refused to calm, and she willed her heart to cease its incessant beating.

Stealing from his own church—not his church but God's church. The alarm racing through her body shouldn't surprise her. If he robbed and killed the people of this town, would he not take their money from the collection plate?

For once she wished she were a lady lawman or a Pinkerton. Why, she'd arrest him this very instant. She'd march into that little room and pronounce him a murderer and a thief.

"Audra, dear, have you been waiting long?" Christopher closed the door of the small room and interrupted her contemplations.

"Not at all." How could he look so innocent? And his voice sounded quiet and calm, like a pastor's. It sickened her.

He held up the familiar leather bag. "This task was left to me today. Do remind me to take this to the bank later."

She smiled and stood. "I can take it for you. It will give me an errand to do."

"Thank you. This is my week to get paid, and I want money there to cover my salary."

His last words burned inside her. All she managed was another smile to keep from screaming at him for dipping his hands into the collection plate.

"You look lovely this morning." He offered her his arm. "We have a dinner invitation. This is a family who gives generously, and we don't want to keep them waiting."

What an incorrigible man.

&

Caleb punched his fist into his palm. He'd rather punch his fist through the side of Jed's barn, but nothing would come from it but a broken hand. He felt weak, helpless, and frustrated. Jed had ridden to Denver to see the governor and hadn't returned. What had taken him so long? Caleb should have gone, too. After all, he was the man with the questionable reputation. He held little hope that Governor Eaton would believe his story. With all the wanted posters, the truth looked far from Earnest, Colorado.

At this very moment what bothered him the most was Naomi's news from Sunday morning church. Chris had announced his marriage to Audra for Sunday, July 9. He knew Audra would refuse to go through with it, but she was in an uncomfortable, even perilous, position. The whole situation with Audra and his brother's plan to fake his own death and leave her a widow heated his blood to boiling.

So far, Caleb had spent every spare minute with his eyes on Earnest and their pastor. Nothing had happened yet. Chris may have decided he had enough money and to give up robbing folks. That didn't take away from the fact he'd committed crimes against good people.

A figure in the doorway captured his attention. "Naomi, I'm on my way," he said.

"Keeping vigil on your brother?"

He nodded. "I expect his Sunday afternoons are spent at some poor unsuspecting person's house for dinner, but I can't take any chances."

"I figured as such. Do you need anything before you leave?"

"No, ma'am. I do appreciate the news about Chris and Audra."

"She doesn't have much time."

"Why did she give him four weeks?" Caleb asked. "It doesn't make sense."

"I imagine she wants him to think the date has something to do with her livelihood. Chris stole her money, except for a little he overlooked, and she doesn't have any income. Now, don't you go thinking she will go through with a wedding so she can survive, 'cause that's not what I'm saying."

"What are you saying?" Caleb asked.

"He's going to make life miserable for her when she backs out, and so will every member of his congregation. But that's not the answer. Don't you understand?"

Realization hit him like a bolt of lightning. "She purposely set herself up to find the evidence in four weeks."

Naomi nodded. "If things aren't resolved by the time of the wedding, she'll find herself a job and do just fine. But by that time she will have lost Christopher's confidence and the hope of helping you."

"I'd have given her money." His words sounded angrier than he intended. "And I never wanted her to help me."

"She's a strong-willed girl, and she's proud. I know she approached the owner of the general store and the boarding-house for work, but neither of them had a job for her." Naomi sighed. "She told me she had the qualifications to teach school."

"I'd like to see her teaching. I think she'd do a fine job."

Naomi walked to where he stood and handed him the food. "God will triumph over this. He will not let Christopher go free and leave you to suffer."

Caleb pressed his lips together. "I want to believe the same thing, and I understand His ways are best." He leaned against the side of a stall and uncovered the plate. "I'd gladly give my life for my brother, if it were any situation other than this. In fact, I'd die right now if this would bring him to his knees." He shrugged. "Maybe that is the answer."

"I hope not." A tear slid down Naomi's round cheek.

"I'm not a brave man, Naomi. Not a real smart one either. But I do know God has a perfect plan."

"Do you trust Him to see you through this to the end?"

He straightened. "Yes, Naomi. I know if I'm looking down a hangman's noose or the barrel of a rifle, He's with me."

"With your kind of faith, this will work out for the best."

He wrapped one arm around her and pulled her to his side. "I pray so." The smell of roast pork tugged at his stomach. "Thanks for taking care of me.

"You're welcome. I wonder if you should be having a conversation with Audra."

He raised a brow. "Why?"

"Because you love her, and she loves you."

He hesitated. How much of his heart dare he confess to this woman? "If my name is cleared, I will approach Audra. Until then, I am a wanted man who can offer nothing but a life on the run."

"Surely there is a place where you two could live in peace."

He smiled. "You are talking like a mother. At least I think so, 'cause I never knew mine." He wiped the tears from her cheeks. "The only safe place for a wanted man is a grave. I will not give up on this fight—not now or ever."

"I understand, and I'm being a silly old woman who loves you like a son."

"We're just stuck, aren't we?" With those words he winked and moved to saddle his horse. He meant those endearing words. A minute more and he'd be behaving like a kid instead of a grown man, crying on her shoulder. Odd how feeling alone made a man vulnerable to his feelings.

"Be careful. Jed should be home on Tuesday."

"I will. I'll check in with both of you that evening."

"Watch out. I don't trust one of the ranch hands—Les."

Caleb sighed. "I'll make sure it's late—like an outlaw."

On Tuesday morning at breakfast, Christopher stated he needed to visit a family and would be gone most of the day. "Those folks have a sick mama. She's not doing well at all. I'm afraid she won't make it."

"May I go along? I could visit with the children. Cook and wash clothes. Do whatever needs to be done." Audra sensed he was lying, and this should prove it.

"I don't think so. You might get sick, too." He smiled. "I want my bride to stay healthy."

"But what about you? The town needs a pastor in one piece."

"I'll be fine. I've done this for a while now, and I haven't caught a thing."

She tilted her head and did her best to manage a quivering smile. "How dear of you to think of me. What is the family's name, and I'll pray for them?"

He leaned across the table and lifted her hand into his. "Sweetheart, you don't know these people. They seldom come to church. Never mind their names, but I'm sure they could use your prayers."

"Most certainly." *Why do I think there isn't a sick mother or a needy family? Christopher, you are simply making this up and making things worse for yourself. God knows what you are doing. You can't hide your lies from Him.* Suddenly a little whisper told her she had not been praying for Christopher. He truly needed the Lord's hand to touch his life.

"Don't look so distraught," he said. "We will make plenty of calls together in the years to come."

"I'm being silly, aren't I?"

"I rather enjoy it."

"Do you suppose tomorrow afternoon you could give me a tour of the parsonage? I really want to see what our home looks like." She paused. "I've wanted to ask you all week—it does not look appropriate, does it?"

"Shall I ask one of the women from church to join us?"

"Naomi?" she asked.

"If it pleases you. I always enjoy talking to Jed." He leaned in closer. "The sheriff suspects the Masterses may know Caleb's whereabouts."

Audra covered her mouth. "Surely not! I'd. . .I'd have discovered it while living there."

He patted her hand still encased in his. "Do not alarm yourself, Audra. I'm sure Sheriff Reynolds's information came from an unreliable source." He released her hand and pulled out a pocket watch—a fine gold one. Probably stolen.

"What time are you leaving?" She offered a sad smile and hated herself for it.

He replaced the watch and tilted back on his chair. "Are you missing me already?"

"I believe so."

"I'm sorry, but I'm leaving shortly after breakfast. How are you spending your day?"

"I might go riding. Close to town of course."

Christopher frowned then finished his coffee. "Don't let the outlines of the buildings get beyond you."

"Don't worry about me. I've learned to be careful." Every word sounded as twisted as his. *Dear Lord, let this be over soon.*

As soon as Christopher left her at the boardinghouse, Audra ascended the stairs to her room. All the while she prayed for Christopher. Once in her room, she dropped to her knees.

Forgive me, Lord, for not asking You to lead Christopher from his sin. Pierce his heart with Your sword of truth. Unite the brothers in a bond of love and forgiveness. Oh, how I long for all of this to be over.

She changed into a riding skirt, one Naomi had sewn for her when she stayed with the couple. Audra had no intentions of using a sidesaddle, and the split skirt often worn by ranchers' wives suited her just fine. Slipping her fingers under the curtain, she peered out through the side of the window and watched Christopher stride toward the livery. He spoke to everyone he met. She admitted he did play the part well. No wonder the entire town believed Caleb rode the outlaw trail.

The moment Audra saw him disappear to retrieve his horse and wagon, she rushed down the stairs and out the front door to the general store across the street. Once inside, she feigned interest in a couple of bonnets artfully placed near the store's window. While she gingerly touched a blue and yellow laced one, she saw Christopher drive the wagon toward the parsonage. Moments later she made her way to the livery.

Papa had shown her how to bridle and saddle a horse when she turned ten years old. Thank goodness, for she needed to hurry, and waiting for the stable boy tried her patience. She led the mare that Jed allowed her to borrow from the livery. She walked the horse toward the parsonage and waited a good distance behind until she saw Christopher leave.

She followed Christopher for over two hours. The wagon ambled west toward the hills that led to the Rockies. She had a difficult time believing a family lived in this secluded area. As usual, the sights and sounds of nature were breathtaking, but she dare not let anything divert her from the task at hand. Once the road wound around the hills, she found it easier to keep a safe pace behind him. He veered the wagon to the right. Audra dismounted and led the mare. From the looks of the thick underbrush, the wagon could not go much further. Up ahead, she saw the wagon and horse—without Christopher.

Audra tied her mare to a sapling and crept closer. Her heart beat so furiously she feared the sound would give her away. Her foot stepped on a stick, and it cracked like rifle fire. She held her breath and anticipated seeing Christopher emerge from the trees, demanding why she'd trailed him.

In the distance she saw him disappear on foot around a curve. The sensible part of her said to ride back to Earnest. The part of her that cared for Caleb and all those who'd been hurt by Christopher's actions spurred her on. She continued up a winding path, stealing behind brush and trees.

If he discovered her, she had no weapon. Stupid! Even if Caleb had denied ever making such an accusation, she certainly claimed it now. A horse neighed. Audra stole behind a juniper tree. There ahead, Christopher rode a pewter-colored stallion. She clutched her heart and silently begged it not to explode from her chest. He headed down the path straight toward her. If he didn't find her, he'd find Jed's mare. She imagined her death would be blamed on Caleb.

As Christopher grew closer, she saw he'd changed clothes. Audra held her breath. He wore the same clothes he'd worn the day he robbed the stage and shot one of the drivers. About fifty feet away from her, he turned south. Four other men rode alongside him—the same men she'd seen before. One of them was the foul-smelling man who had sat across from her and Papa. Another she recognized from Jed's ranch—Les.

"You're right on time," Christopher said.

"We're always where we need to be," the foul-smelling man said.

"Right, Hawk. Do we need to go over what we're doing?" Christopher asked. "That stage is due in thirty minutes, and it's carrying cash from Denver."

"We know what we're doing," another man said.

"Remember this is my last job." Christopher laughed.

"Yeah. I hear you're getting married," Hawk said and spit tobacco juice several feet.

"Not for long. Soon as I say I do, I'm faking the preacher's death and sending half the state after Caleb while I'm taking life easy in Mexico."

The other men laughed.

"You gonna leave the prettiest girl in these parts?" Les asked. "She'd sure tempt me."

Audra squeezed her eyes shut to keep from sobbing. Every muscle in her body tightened. Would any of the townsfolk believe what she'd heard and seen? Suddenly an unseen hand gripped her mouth.

thirteen

"Audra, you're too close. Chris and his men will find you—both of us."

She willed her body to cease its trembling, but every part of her quivered like a fall leaf. She was safe. Caleb held her, not one of Christopher's men. He smelled of leather and the freshness of morning, not the wild desperation of evil men. The violation she feared had not occurred—would not as long as she obeyed Caleb.

"I'm going to release you. Take my hand, and let's get back out of sight." His breath tickled her ear. "Move quietly. Watch where you step."

She nodded, but still her legs felt like soft jelly. His hand lifted from her mouth, and she breathed in and out in an effort to calm herself. Somehow she rested her hand into his and let him lead her farther into the brush. She did her best to walk on the soft earth, but her footsteps broke through the silence like a crack of thunder.

Caleb stopped and turned to her. "Easy," he whispered. "I'm right here."

A chill raced up her arm, and she knew for certain Caleb Windsor cared as much for her as she did for him. How terribly sad for two unlikely people to be denied their affections. Before this horrible experience came to a close, one of the two Windsor brothers may be killed—most likely the man she loved.

A few moments later, Christopher and his men rode by en route to where the stage cleared an open stretch of land. Staring ahead to where she'd stood only a moment ago, Audra saw how easily she could have been discovered. The thought caused her to shudder.

"I am terribly foolish," she said. "If not for you, they would. . .have found me."

He squeezed her hand lightly then grasped her shoulders. His rigid features spoke for him. "Don't you ever do anything like this again. Luckily I saw you before they did."

"I didn't realize—"

"Hush and listen to me. You, little lady, are allowed to keep Chris company with the idea you might hear something that will help us. No following him. Ever. No creeping around like a lawman. Ever. Do you understand every word I've said?"

She nodded, still too frightened to argue.

"Don't think I haven't considered wiring your folks about the danger here."

She cringed and her stubbornness rose to the surface. "You wouldn't dare."

The menacing gaze emitting from his wide eyes didn't require a reply.

"I want to do more. It's important to me," she said.

"Like today? Promise me this idiocy is over, or I will have Jed wire your folks as soon as he can ride into Earnest."

Feeling like a trapped animal she agreed. "I'll do what you say." *Maybe.*

His arms dropped to his sides. "Good. I imagine you heard the conversation between Chris and his men."

"I did." She took a deep breath. "Everything is true. He actually intends to marry me, fake his death, and blame it on you."

"I'm sorry, Audra."

"Don't be. I know he's wretched, and you told me this before, but each time I learn something new for myself, I get angrier than I thought possible." She gasped and focused her attention on him. "Your poor father. He will be grief-stricken. He always talks about how proud he is of both of you."

Caleb said nothing, only peered back at her. His wrinkled brow told her he didn't need a reminder of his father.

"I treasure Pastor Windsor," Audra said. "He gives more to

others than anyone I know." *And you are so much like him.* "He'll be so upset."

"Do you really think he doesn't suspect something? That Chris hasn't told him about my unlawful activities?"

When she paused to consider the question, her heart plummeted. "You mean he may already believe you are an outlaw?"

"Why wouldn't he?"

She nodded slowly. "Are you telling me it wouldn't do any good for you to contact him, have him come out here, and try to convince Chris to abandon his ways?"

"Our father is already hurting—has been for a long time. Why make it any worse until this is settled?" He paused and expelled a labored breath. "Audra, your suggestion may be a good idea. I haven't written him in a few years. He might take notice and listen."

"You're right, and then if he came out here—"

"He could see for himself." Caleb nodded. Lines deepened around his eyes.

She glanced about and drank in a faint fragrance of wildflowers. A soft breeze rustled through the treetops. She stood next to a man she loved and couldn't utter a word about it. *Talk about something other than Chris or their father.* "This is such beautiful country."

"Torn apart by greedy men."

She forced a lump back down her throat. "I can't believe Les is a part of those men, too," she said. "He's spying on everything that goes on at the Masterses' ranch."

"Naomi suspected him and warned me."

"I remembered Hawk from the stage with Papa and me. He reminded me of a pig."

Caleb lifted a brow. "You recognized him? I caught him at Jed and Naomi's posing as a bounty hunter. He's the one who said you'd gone to the sheriff about me hiding out at their ranch."

She tilted her head. "Who else is in on this?"

"I hope no one. Those other two fellas riding with Chris are strangers. No doubt keeping low. Jed's supposed to be back from Denver today. It will be a miracle if Governor Eaton swallows his story—even so, he'll need proof."

"I'll testify." An idea enveloped her, a wonderful idea. "I can go to Denver tomorrow, and I'll tell the governor the whole story."

"Absolutely not."

Heat flooded her face. "Why? I witnessed Chris and his men today. You need my testimony to clear your name."

"Who is going to protect you until then? How are you going to get to Denver without Chris coming after you? And I guarantee my brother won't be alone. What will be your reason for leaving Earnest?" He crossed his arms over his chest. "Without evidence, it's the pastor and the sheriff's word against a young woman who hasn't been in town long enough to make friends—except for the couple who are allegedly hiding out an outlaw."

"You obviously don't have much faith in my persuasive abilities with Christopher or the governor's ability to discern the truth."

"Audra, please. I want this thing ended more than anyone, but my brother is on the winning side unless we find the money and stolen goods."

Her shoulders fell along with her optimism. "I wish I knew what to do."

"You can take the next stage back to Nebraska."

"I can't." She dare not tell him of her love. He'd force her back to Nebraska for sure—just to keep her safe.

"I know Chris stole your money. I'll pay the fare."

"I don't want your money!" *Don't let your heart betray you.*

Silence settled thickly, like the dead calm before a violent storm.

"Let's not quarrel," Caleb said.

She understood. Angry words solved nothing. "All right."

"Will you go back home?"

"No. Not now or ever." Audra's heart hammered against her chest.

"Why? When there's nothing here for you but a town full of deceit?"

Mama always said what a person didn't say often shouted louder than the words coming from their mouth. At the time, Audra thought her mother spoke in riddles. Now she understood. Loving Caleb Windsor meant more to her than a life of peace and comfort in Nebraska. If he guessed her heart, he'd have one more burden—whether he shared in the feelings or not. She dare not tell him all the reasons why she had to stay. "I made a commitment to begin a new life here."

"A life with my brother, the pastor."

"I understood right from the beginning that a marriage might not be part of my future with Christopher. I came prepared to find work. Why are you anxious to have me gone?"

"So you don't get yourself hurt."

She'd succeeded in irritating him again. "We're bickering."

"And I need to leave."

She peered into his rugged face. "Are you taking out after Chris?"

"I want to see if I can stop the robbery. At least find out where he's taking the money."

"I'd like to—"

His narrowed gaze stopped her. "Can you find your way back to town?"

She nodded, and they walked to her horse. Many things raced through her mind, none of which she could voice. Every time she saw him could be the last. Every time she took a glimpse into his midnight blue eyes and nearly drowned in them could be nothing more than a memory. His deep gentle voice could become a haunting recollection. Oh, to tell Caleb she loved him. Taking a deep breath, she grabbed the reins and allowed him to help her swing up into the saddle.

"If you don't keep your word, I will escort you to Nebraska myself," he said.

And she knew he meant every word. "I understand. I'll remember every word you say. God be with you."

⋙

Trying to talk sense into Audra lessened Caleb's chances of making it to the stage before the robbery. If only he could arrive in time to warn the driver, even if it meant posing as Chris and ordering the stage to return to Denver. The thought of another killing spurred him on faster. What a nest of rattlers this had become.

By the time he caught up with his brother, the stage ambled on to Earnest with a little less money, and hopefully no one hurt. Caleb trailed the outlaws until they split up, his brother heading back alone to where he'd left the wagon.

Anger moved through Caleb like a brush fire. He desperately wanted to get the money back and return it to those it belonged to. The truth made him hotter than Naomi's cookstove. Who'd he give it to? The driver, who'd gladly unload his rife on him? The sheriff? The bounty-hunter outlaw?

Lord, I'm wandering like a blind man in a snake pit.

While he lingered behind Chris, an image of Audra refused to let him go. As much as he wanted to shake the stubbornness out of her, he'd rather pull her into his arms and never let her go. How could one little lady drive a man to distraction? He prayed for her protection and for her to get on the next stage back to Nebraska. It no longer mattered that he'd never see her again; she'd be safe from Chris. Each time they were together, he fought telling her how he felt and how he dreamed of the two of them having a life free of the nightmares chasing them. With a shrug he pushed her from his mind and stuck to his brother's trail.

Back at the wagon site, Sheriff Reynolds waited nearby. He took a long drink from his canteen and waved at Chris. "Thought I'd give you an escort back to town." He pushed his hat back on his head.

"You don't trust me?"

"Not when you'd pin a murder on your own brother."

Chris laughed and patted his saddlebags. "Got it all right here. Double-crossing a sheriff doesn't sound smart to me." He swung down from his horse. "Glad you came by. I wouldn't put it past Caleb to stop me along the road and hand out some brotherly advice. Lately he's been real upset at what I've been doing."

"That sure would make it easier for me. Lynch the thief and fill my pockets."

"Save us all some heartache."

The sheriff eyed Chris with a sneer. "Doesn't it bother you what you've done to Caleb?"

"Nah. He's always been a fool. I'm the one with the brains."

"What about acting like a preacher?"

"I learned how all that was done from my old man. You going soft on me?"

"Not in the least. Just wondering. What about Miss Lenders?"

Chris eased back in the saddle. "Haven't decided what to do with her yet. I'm considering taking her with me to Mexico."

So brother does have a weak spot when it comes to Audra. She should be safe around him.

"You think she'd go?" Sheriff Reynolds asked.

"I think she'd do anything I asked her." Chris chuckled. "I have a way with the ladies." He threw the saddlebags over his left shoulder.

"Why don't you leave her here? Just think of those dark-haired gals in Mexico."

"I prefer the one with sun-colored hair."

"Don't tell me you want to take up with the woman?" the sheriff asked.

Chris failed to respond. Instead, he dismounted and hitched up the horse and wagon. "I said nothing of the sort. She'd be a sight better company than you are."

"Bad idea if you ask me. She doesn't come across like the type who'd say nothing about the way you get your money."

"Shut up, Reynolds. You take care of covering for me, and I'll take care of my personal business."

Caleb wanted to ride into the open and lay his brother flat on the ground—his usual response to Chris's actions. Odd, Caleb had never struck his brother even as a boy. It didn't matter. Chris had no right talking about Audra as though she were a faithful dog or a good horse. *Lord, how did my brother get so bad? Is his meanness my fault? Did my taking all the blame for him cause this trouble?*

"So this is the last job we pull together?" the sheriff asked.

"I think so. Not unless you get wind of a money shipment."

"Not likely. The governor wired me about the robberies and offered an armed escort. After today, he'll follow through for sure."

Chris nodded. "Guess we're done then. We'll divide this up a few days before the wedding."

"Why wait so long?"

"I don't want to risk those guys waving around extra cash and folks getting suspicious before I'm long gone."

fourteen

Caleb trailed Chris and the sheriff back to Earnest. He was furious with the conversation he'd overheard, but as usual what could he do? He rode out toward the Masterses' ranch in hopes Jed had made it home from Denver. Might be some good news there. Long after the sun went down, he rapped on Jed and Naomi's door. Les and the other ranch hands appeared to have settled in for the night. He heard one of them mention a card game and figured they'd be busy for a long time.

"Come on in, son," Jed said barely above a whisper. "Been expecting you."

Naomi pulled the curtains shut then uncovered a plate of food on the stove left from supper. She pointed to an empty chair at the table and set a hearty helping of stew in front of him. "How was your day?"

Caleb eased into the chair and stretched out his long legs. "All right." Tired best described him: physically and mentally. He'd rather mend fences from sunup to sundown seven days a week than keep an eye out for Chris and worry about what might happen to those he cared about. Lately he felt like David running from King Saul. Unfortunately, Caleb didn't have all of David's fine traits—only the similarity of running from a man who wrongfully pursued him.

"You look plumb worn out, worse than Jed." Naomi poured him a glass of cool buttermilk.

"Why don't you eat before you tell us about the past few days?" Jed said. "I had a fair meeting with the governor, and I'm hoping some good will come of it." He turned to Naomi. "I could use a glass of buttermilk, too, and another piece of that berry pie."

Caleb rested one arm on the table. His stomach complained of not eating since breakfast, and the tantalizing smells nearly did him in. But his mind raced with questions that held no answers, and he desperately craved them. He stuck his fork into a chunk of beef, tender enough for a baby to eat. Once he'd eaten about half of his food, he glanced at Jed. "I trailed Chris this morning and found out he had plans to rob the stage again."

Naomi groaned.

"I didn't get there in time to stop it, nor could I figure out where they hid the money except Chris took it with him into town. Don't believe anyone was hurt." He picked up a biscuit and heaped apple butter between the thick layers. "Good food, Naomi. Thanks." He paused. "Sheriff met him back in the hills, and together they headed to Earnest."

"So he must keep it at the parsonage," Jed said.

"Most likely. But we have another problem, almost as bad."

"Can't imagine things getting worse." Jed took a long drink of the buttermilk and a generous bite of pie.

"I caught Audra trailing after him, too. She nearly got caught before I yanked her out of there. Don't want to think of what Chris and his men might have done to her."

Jed's eyes widened, and he put down his fork. "What in the world was she doing out there? I thought she understood 'nothing dangerous.' "

"Her foolishness is going to get her killed." Caleb swirled the buttermilk in his glass. "I threatened to wire her father about the goings-on here, even told her I'd escort her back to Nebraska if she ever did anything like that again."

"Did she promise to behave herself?" Jed tugged at his mustache, now frosted in white. "She isn't afraid of anything, is she?"

"I'm thankful she's all right, but she's a woman in love, looking for a way to help her man." Naomi nodded in Caleb's direction.

Caleb looked up. "Where did you get such a crazy notion?"

"By looking at her," Naomi said. "Isn't that right, Jed?"

Jed sighed and pointed a finger at Caleb. "Sure is plain to me."

What can I say? I've seen something akin to love in Audra's eyes, too, or maybe I wanted to see it. "Doesn't matter what you saw or thought you saw, nothing can happen between us as long as I'm a wanted man."

"You're right, son." Jed pushed back his empty plate and stood. Sticking his fingers under his suspenders, he paced the room. "This business keeps getting more complicated."

"I think Chris may have found some feelings for her, too."

Naomi wiggled her shoulders as though she'd just tasted something nasty. "He doesn't know how to care for anyone but himself. How could he find feelings for Audra?"

Caleb suddenly lost his appetite. "From what Chris said to the sheriff, I'd say he's having second thoughts about leaving Audra behind."

Jed cleared his throat. "You mean he's talking about staying in Earnest?"

He shook his head. "Considering taking her with him to Mexico."

"Well, she'd never agree." Naomi planted her hands on her hips. "My lands, when will this get settled?"

"Soon." Jed startled him with the conviction in his voice.

"What did Governor Eaton say?" Caleb asked. "Best tell me. It's been worrying at me since you left."

Jed eased back into his chair, his round stomach rubbing against the table. "I wouldn't say the news is bad. It simply could be better. I talked to the governor—explained it all. He said we needed evidence to clear you."

"Did you tell him how long we've been looking?" Caleb felt the age-old frustration creep into his bones.

"Yeah. He's sending a man from his office to do a little snooping around. If you get arrested, he'll wire the governor to make sure you get a fair trial."

"You mean a fair hangin'?"

"Hush, Caleb." Naomi's forehead crinkled. "One more person on our side is a welcome thing."

He stretched back his neck. Tired, so tired. "The President himself could be on our side, but without proof of my innocence we have nothing." Silence grated the room. Outside one of the dogs barked. "I need to get inside the parsonage. The money has to be hidden there. In fact, I have an idea since Miss Audra is so eager to help."

"You're not going to ask her to do anything outlandish, are you?" Naomi said.

"Nope." Caleb laughed, despite the circumstances. "I thought you could invite Audra and Chris out here for dinner. Keep them late, insist they stay long after dark. That'll give me plenty of time to search the parsonage."

"Now I'm being left out of the excitement," Jed said and picked up his pipe. "I'd love to find all the stolen money."

"You're too old for excitement," Naomi said. "You can spend your time thinking of things to talk about with Christopher, since he's one of your favorite people."

Jed scowled. "Old woman, you're getting feistier as the years go by."

She kissed the top of his baldhead. "You wouldn't have it any other way."

Jed grinned and winked at Caleb. "This is what you have to look forward to."

Sun-kissed hair and wide blue eyes rested in his mind. *Life with Audra would be a glimpse of heaven. . .if I live to court her proper.*

❧

Audra thought if she shared one more miserable meal with Christopher, she'd be sick. And all over him, too. Goodness, she'd gotten surly. He looked up from his fried chicken and smiled. *Wonder why he's being exceptionally nice?* Every day brought them closer to their wedding day—she planned to stand him up at the altar by riding out of town in the opposite direction.

"Heard from Jed Masters today," Christopher said.

She gave him her full attention. "I wish he'd stopped into the boardinghouse."

"He was in a hurry. They invited us to dinner tomorrow night."

Her smile came naturally. "Wonderful. I miss them."

"We'll have a pleasant evening of it, my dear. Not too late, though. The thought of driving back after dark with my brother on the loose doesn't sit well with me."

She startled. "How horrid of him to stop us on the road. Neither of us has anything of value for him to steal. The thief already took my money."

"Don't put it past him. He's done worse. I'm sure he'd like nothing better than to ruin our wedding day."

She bit her tongue to keep from giving him a piece of her mind. Pleasantries with him were becoming increasingly difficult.

"I wish he'd take all the money he's stolen and leave the state," he said.

"Where do you think he'd go?" she asked.

"South America is my guess. He could live there like a king."

Like you plan to do? She picked at her food. "What does the sheriff think?"

"We've talked about it. Oh, Audra, I hate to worry your pretty little head with talk of catching a criminal."

She wondered if they'd planned to trap Caleb—force him into the open.

"I'm sure we will be fine tomorrow night." He wiped his fingers on a napkin. "I'm not concerned about me, only you." He finished the potatoes and corn on his plate. "Are you a good cook?"

Cook? She considered his question. How tempting to tell him no or offer to prepare him a terrible meal. He'd probably want fried rattlesnake. "I'm not sure how good, but Mama and Papa never complained."

"I suspect I'll be looking like Jed in no time at all."

Can't get plump in prison. "Oh my, a portly pastor, but a jolly one." She covered her mouth to suppress a laugh. "What is your favorite?"

"Fried chicken and cobbler. I love a good apple cobbler with a thick crust and sweet cream."

Audra laughed, but not for the reason he suspected. "Hmm, with mounds of sugar sprinkled on top."

"Yes, ma'am." He leaned in closer. "I'm also looking forward to children—lots of little girls who look like their mama." His gaze lingered on her face, the type that made her feel as though she needed to slap him. "All with silky, sun-colored hair and light blue eyes. I'd have a whole household of my Audra."

She blushed scarlet and felt the heat rising from her neck. Did Christopher have to continue lying so? It was a wonder the good Lord didn't throw a bolt of lightning his way. "You embarrass me, Christopher," she whispered. "What would people say if they heard you?"

He gave her an impish grin. "They'd say there's a man in love who's planning his future."

Audra shivered. For a moment she believed him. The impossibility of ever having a relationship with Christopher made her shudder. He was a killer, a liar, a thief. And he cared not to hide his improper thoughts. With all he'd done. With her feelings for Caleb. Did he think she was that naïve? This had to be a game for him, a diversion to pass the time until he left Earnest for Mexico.

"I've made you speechless with my comments," he said. "But I have a surprise."

She lifted her gaze, dreading his next words. "I can hardly wait."

"If you'd still like to see the parsonage Saturday morning, one of the members will be helping me repair the church's roof, so it'd be proper."

"What about your sermon?"

"It's finished."

"I'd love it," she said. "Can I do a little exploring to see where you have things stored and such?"

"Of course. I like my home neat and orderly, so I don't think you will find fault with my housekeeping."

She forced a laugh. She remembered the clean, folded handkerchief he used to wipe the blood from her finger. "I hadn't thought anything of the sort."

"If the parsonage suits you, we could move up the wedding date."

"You are teasing me. Admit it, Christopher. The wedding date will be here before we know it, and probably before I'm completely ready."

"If I had the money, I'd whisk you away to someplace where no one would ever bother us. What do you say? Back East? Europe? To South America like my wayward brother is probably planning?"

"All on a poor pastor's wages?" She leaned closer and pretended to cling to his witty conversation. How she'd relish the opportunity to hear him admit his guilt. "You and I would have to rob all the good people of Earnest to afford such luxury."

fifteen

Mid afternoon on Thursday, Audra and Christopher rode the wagon to Jed and Naomi's. She'd slept little the night before thinking about seeing her friends. They hadn't been attending church lately, and she had mixed feelings about it. Audra wanted to tell them about Saturday's plans to explore the parsonage while Christopher busied himself with the church's roof repair. Giddiness swelled in her, the first real source of joy she'd felt since coming to Colorado. She pictured herself telling Caleb she'd found the money. Soon he'd enjoy the freedom of living on his ranch without fear of being arrested—or worse.

"You're happy, aren't you?" Christopher asked. "I hope you are finally putting aside the stage robbery."

Startled, Audra scrambled for words. "At the moment, yes. I pray justice will soon rule Earnest and not this cloud of fear."

"I agree, except that means my brother will be suffering the consequences of his actions."

"All evil men need to understand their ways will catch up with them." To keep from displaying her frustration, she chose to discard the subject of Earnest's unrest. "Colorado is so beautiful. I'm glad this is my new home, and I love Naomi and Jed. They are like parents to me."

"Yes, this territory suits you well. Your cheeks have a nice rosy color, and I can see in your eyes how much you appreciate the mountains."

Since she'd moved into the boardinghouse, Christopher had been a perfect gentleman. To her it seemed like Christopher was two men, and the realization frightened her, for at any moment he could change into a man who was capable of hurting her and others.

"I've never told you I love you," he said.

Those were the last words she wanted to hear. She wished he'd pick up the horse's pace. Nervousness pounded at her temples. "Please wait. We are barely more than strangers."

"I think my heart was smitten the first time I saw you."

"Love takes time," she said. "And we are friends, growing closer every day."

His shoulders lifted and fell. "I want us to declare a mutual love on our wedding day."

She smiled. Her pledge to help end his lawlessness contrasted with his tenderness toward her. The momentary kindness nibbled at her conscience. Had she become no better than he by leading him to believe she cared for him? In any event, she refused to tell him what he wanted to hear. Enough lies had passed between them without her adding another.

"Are you shy about matters of the heart?" he asked.

"Yes, I imagine so." A reminder of her feelings for Caleb seized her, the devotion she must keep hidden.

"Then I'll wait. Hearing your love for me is worth the wait, for a hundred years if necessary. For you are truly a treasure. My father hand-selected you for me, and he did a fine job."

She breathed the freshness of the afternoon air, anxious to be at Jed and Naomi's. Tonight she could be with friends, and for a few hours she'd be relieved of dealing with Christopher. With an inward sigh, she realized Caleb had borne this load for years. The least she could do was endeavor to help him clear his name.

"I've been thinking about a trip for our honeymoon," he said.

She turned to him, grateful for a reprieve from the previous topic. "Where did you have in mind?"

"Mexico."

Panic gripped her heart. "What about your church?"

"I could get a good man to watch over things until we returned."

"How long would we be gone?"

He grinned. "Maybe forever. I hear Mexico is a beautiful country."

"You mean establish a new church there?"

"Whatever you want, Audra."

&

Caleb spied Christopher and Audra leaving Earnest in the afternoon. Envy twisted his heart, because he wanted to be seated beside her. As he watched his brother turn to Audra, another thought consumed him—a protective one. His brother and Audra would be alone all the way to the Masterses' ranch and all the way back. He had to believe Chris had no intentions of harming her, and the conversation he'd heard between his brother and the sheriff was not another lie. If Chris truly had feelings for Audra, then he'd honor and respect her.

Wrestling with his own need to find proof of his innocence and to keep Audra safe, he decided to follow the wagon then double back to the parsonage. Granted, he'd have to hurry in his search, but he could manage it. As soon as he finished there, he'd race back to the Masterses' ranch and make sure his brother behaved himself in escorting Audra home.

Beneath a starless night, Caleb stole to the rear of the parsonage. He crawled through a bedroom window and pulled the curtains shut. In the dark, he drew a candle from inside his shirt and lit it. Everything in the room looked perfect, but that was Chris. When they were younger, the two boys argued more about Chris's insistence to keep things in order than anything else. Caleb believed the stolen money and other goods were stacked neatly in a spot where no one suspected. His gaze swept around the room. Where did he begin?

Caleb yanked on a dresser drawer. It squeaked and crashed to the floor. The sound shook his resolve. He refused to move, certain the sheriff waited in the next room.

Why am I going through my brother's house like a thief? He bent and picked up the drawer and slid it into place. Standing in the middle of the bedroom, he blew out the candle. He'd become as low as a snake's belly. His friends protected him. The woman he loved risked being hurt. Why? If he trusted God, then he needed to listen for His direction. Alone in the parsonage, he realized his hurt and angry feelings combined with his desire to see Chris suffer didn't glorify God.

With the curtains shoved back into place, he crawled out through the window, secured his horse, and rode toward the Masterses' ranch. He had plenty of solitude between Earnest and the ranch to seek the Lord's forgiveness for the things he'd thought and planned regarding his brother. High time he followed God's steps instead of expecting God to follow his.

❧

Audra learned from Naomi about the plan to lengthen supper and the after-dinner conversation. Surely Caleb knew where to search in the parsonage. She'd be stumbling around like a blind person.

Later that evening when she and Christopher finally said their good-byes, the lack of a full moon forced them to light the wagon lanterns.

"I know you wanted to leave earlier," Audra said. "I suppose I should apologize."

"Never mind a bit," Christopher said. "We got started a little later in the afternoon than I expected, and I wanted you to have a good visit with the Masterses."

His good-natured mannerisms struck a guilty chord in Audra. The Christopher she met in the middle of the dusty road on the way to Earnest was selfish and cruel. But of late, he hid it well. The mask didn't make up for the horrible crimes he committed. She simply saw his charming side—the sweetness that the members of his church loved and appreciated.

When Audra was a little girl, a neighbor had the most loveable dog. One day it got sick, and the dog's disposition changed. When the neighbor tried to feed the animal, it bit him. Christopher reminded her of that dog. He had the abilities to serve God in the finest capacity. Instead, he maneuvered the innocent to make a profit.

The wagon ambled on as Audra's thoughts floated from the past in Nebraska to today's problems. Always, she lingered on Caleb—dear sweet Caleb who had suffered the most in all of this.

Night sounds lulled her, and she felt her eyelids grow heavy.

"Are you tired?" Christopher asked.

"Very."

"We'll be home soon." He chuckled. "In a few weeks, the boardinghouse will be your old home."

She failed to reply.

"Go ahead and put your head on my shoulder. I'll wake you when we get to town."

"We have a few things to discuss, brother." She recognized Caleb's voice. The wagon came to an abrupt stop.

"Have you been following us?" Christopher's tone spit venom.

"Does it matter? What I have to say won't take long."

Christopher shifted on the wagon seat. "Remember there's a lady present."

"I'm not the one who has a habit of breaking the law to offend her."

"All right, Caleb. Say your piece and leave us alone." Anger laced Christopher's words.

"I've given you plenty of chances to turn yourself in, and nothing's ever changed. You're a lone wolf—too mean to keep company with decent folk. You're a disgrace to our father and to God."

Audra heard the confidence in Caleb. In the past he'd sounded bold, but not courageous.

Christopher laughed. "I think you're talking about yourself."

"The folks around here will soon know the truth about their pastor. Governor Eaton knows what's going on here, and he's not a happy man about it."

"Good! I hope he sends someone to investigate. The

sheriff will welcome a hand. Earnest needs to be rid of the likes of you."

"Now that's a peculiar statement since the sheriff is in on this with you."

Audra saw Chris reach behind him. In the next instant, a revolver flashed in the dim light. "You are a threat to my future wife. I hate the thought of shooting my own brother, but you give me no choice."

"No!" Audra screamed. "Please, Christopher. Don't do this."

"What's the matter with you? He's a thief and a murderer. Didn't you tell me that you wanted him stopped before we were married?"

"Not anymore. Let the law take care of him." Her heart hammered against her chest.

"Why not now?" Christopher asked.

"Audra, I can handle this," Caleb said. "No need for you to get involved."

Christopher flashed his attention her way. "Are you seeing Caleb? Are you? Is that what this is all about? Are you in this with him? Trying to betray me? Tell me, or I'll pull the trigger now."

"Leave her out of our quarrel," Caleb said. From the corner of her eye, Audra saw Caleb dismount. She dare not take her gaze from Christopher.

"Stop right now." Christopher waved the revolver. "No one will blame me for this. No one. Answer my question, Audra. Are you in love with my brother?"

"You're angry." She willed her mind to clear. "Put the gun away. You don't want to do this. How can you live with shooting your brother?"

"Answer my question now." Christopher lifted the revolver.

"Yes." Her reply echoed across the night. "I do love Caleb. Please put the gun down. I'll do anything you say, but don't hurt him."

Christopher chuckled. "Anything? Marry me like you promised?"

"Whatever you want." She blinked back the tears. "Just don't pull the trigger."

"Audra," Caleb said. "I'd rather be dead than have you married to him."

Caleb's words cut through her heart. She had no choice. Couldn't he see that?

"Caleb, are you in love with her?"

She waited to hear his answer. Her pulse quickened. She feared Christopher would not wait to shoot him. This is not how she wanted to declare her love for Caleb, or hear if he shared the same feelings.

"Yes, I am," Caleb said.

"Hate to disappoint you, but she's mine."

Audra flung her body against Christopher. The gun fired. Caleb struggled with his brother. Both men fell into the dirt and wrestled with the weapon. Another shot fired. She scrambled down from the wagon.

"Stay back, Audra," Caleb said.

She obeyed, not knowing what else to do. Amid the sounds of Christopher's cursing, Caleb finally stood with the revolver in his hand. She seemed to quiver more in seeing he was safe than she had during the scuffle.

"Head on back to town," Caleb said.

Christopher rubbed his jaw. "I'm not finished with this."

"I wish you were. How do you think our father is going to feel when he finds out the truth? Bad enough he thinks I'm the outlaw. Worse yet is to learn you lied and deceived folks in the name of God."

"Leave me alone. I know what I'm doing."

He isn't denying Caleb's accusations.

Christopher climbed back into the wagon. "You going with me?" he asked Audra. "Or have you made your choice?"

She lifted her chin. "Do you think I'd go anywhere with you?"

"I'm not finished with you either. There will come a time when you will beg me to marry you. There's no future with

Caleb—nothing but watching him hang."

"I'll take my chances."

"You could have had a good life with me, Audra. My affections were real."

She watched Christopher pick up the reins and urge the horse toward Earnest. The light shawl wrapped around her shoulders did nothing to stop the chill racing up her arms. She watched until the kerosene lanterns on both sides of the wagon faded into the distance.

"Audra."

She whirled in the direction of Caleb's voice. Without a full moon or stars, she saw only a faint outline of his figure. She despised the conflict between the brothers. Twins were supposed to be closer than regular brothers or sisters. This had to hurt him beyond words. Now he had the burden of a woman in love with him.

"Are you angry with me?" she asked.

"How could I be? I am as much to blame as you are. He asked us questions, and we answered."

"I was so afraid for you. Are you hurt?"

"Nothing that Naomi can't bandage up."

She gasped and stumbled in the dark to his side. She wanted to touch him, make sure Christopher had not hurt him badly. "Are you making light of a serious wound? Did I do this when I pushed Christopher? What can I do?"

"This happened in the scuffle. It's not serious."

Tears seeped from her eyes and trickled down her cheeks. "I never meant. . .it to happen. I didn't even like you. . .in the beginning."

"I understand," he said. "I saw the love in your eyes."

"And I saw it in yours." She wanted to step into his arms, but he gave no indication of wanting her there.

"Until my name is cleared, nothing can happen between us." His voice resounded with conviction. "I cannot hold you or talk about what was said here tonight."

She wanted to tell him she loved him without Christopher

pointing a gun at him, but she had to respect his stand. "I believe a horrible trick has been played on us." She paused and swiped at her wet cheeks. "We need to see Naomi. I have a feeling you are hurt more than what you are saying."

"Can you ride in front of me?"

Panic seized her. "Where are you shot?"

"My shoulder. Left side."

"Shouldn't I help you on and then crawl up behind you?"

"I can manage."

She feared Christopher had aimed for his heart and missed. *Dear Lord, brother against brother? This sounds too much like Papa speaking about the Civil War. Please touch Christopher's heart. He can be a good man. At times he's treated me properly. Right now, I'm asking You for healing—for Caleb's wound and Christopher's heart.*

Audra tucked her dress between her knees and lifted her foot into the stirrup. Caleb attempted to help, but he appeared too weak.

"Give me your hand," she said.

"I'm fine."

"Please, Caleb. Let me do something for you. How can you swing up onto the saddle with your left arm in pain?" He reached up, and she grasped his hand. The sole of his boot scraped against the wooden stirrup. When she pulled on him he groaned and nearly fell. "You can climb up here," she said and refused to release his hand.

The horse reared slightly, and Caleb fell onto the dirt road. "Go after Jed," he said. "Tell him I need help."

sixteen

When Caleb was a kid, a mule kicked him and broke his leg. Nothing had ever hurt him like that since—until tonight when Christopher's revolver fired into his shoulder. Every time his heart beat, a surge of pain nearly took his breath away.

"Lucky for you that bullet went through to the other side," Naomi said. "Instead of cleaning up this hole, I'd be digging out a piece of lead."

"That's comforting." His shoulder throbbed, worse by the minute. He peered up at Naomi. "I know I should be thanking you for this—"

She raised a brow. "Are you complaining about my nursing? Ah, I bet you want Audra to clean and bandage you up. She might be gentler than these rough, calloused hands, but those salty tears of hers might sting a bit."

Naomi's teasing reminded him of Audra's confession earlier. And his own. He couldn't bring himself to look at her for fear he'd melt like butter on a hot day. She'd said little since riding after Jed. Perhaps her mind wrestled with the shooting or the understanding that they both loved each other. How easy it would be to take her into his arms, but how selfish of him to take advantage of her tender feelings.

Although Jed and Naomi sat with them in the kitchen, he needed for Audra to understand the stark reality of living a life on the run. He fixed his gaze on his beloved. "See this blood running down my arm, Audra? Do you remember the way you trembled when Christopher held the gun? That is my life. It will not change until my brother is stopped and my name's cleared." He winced as Naomi dabbed the hole in his shoulder with whiskey poured onto a clean cloth. He'd never had any use for the stuff. His father had called it devil's brew, and by the way it burned his shoulder, Caleb agreed. "If we were together, you'd be bandaging me up, not Naomi. You'd be ripping apart your petticoat for bandages and using creek water for medicine. Our home would be anyplace we could hide. Some farmer's barn that smelled of manure. Or under the stars, where we would pray it didn't rain or snow. If we made it to South America, we'd have to stay there till the day we died and hope the law didn't come after us."

Tears welled in her eyes. She bit her lip, no doubt to stop the sobs. "I know it would be a hard life."

He despised the words coming from his mouth. "Hard? Audra, it's a life not fit for a man, least of all a woman." She stood close enough for him to touch her. How he longed to wipe the tears from her cheeks, weave his fingers through her hair.

"Christopher could have shot you today. I won't have it. The best thing you can do for me is to go back to Nebraska."

She shook her head. "Never. I'm staying here. I will not run from what your brother is doing and allow him to gloat over it."

"Tonight you agreed to marry him, if he didn't shoot me."

Her face paled. "And I would have."

"He could do the same thing again. Don't you see that he will try to get me through you?"

"Then I will hide, too."

Caleb tore his attention away from her and fixed his gaze on Naomi. "Can't you reason with her? Make her see I'm afraid she's going to get hurt."

The lines in Naomi's face deepened. "How can I deny Audra her dreams? I'm an old woman. You are a son to me, and I cannot let you fight this alone either."

"Neither can I." Jed handed Naomi another clean bandage. "We're a ragged sort of family here, Caleb. You have our loyalty whether you want it or not." He clasped his hand onto Caleb's good shoulder. "God is on our side. Admittedly so, we have little chance of success. But with God, justice and truth will win."

Caleb nodded. The pain had weakened him, dulled his judgment. His emotions were tossed. He had to stand firm—for his father, Jed, and Naomi, for Audra, and most of all for God.

Moments passed in silence. He watched Naomi thoroughly clean his shoulder. Good thing Chris's aim was tempered by the dark. A few more inches and that bullet would have pierced his heart.

"I do have an idea," Caleb finally said. "Chris and the sheriff are bent on trapping me, but I think we could set one for them." He turned to Audra. "Would you be willing to go back to the boardinghouse?"

She gasped. Her pale skin grew even whiter. "And give up any chance of seeing you?"

"To help me." He gazed at her. "If it appears you have deserted us, and you must find a place to live before returning to Nebraska, Chris and the sheriff will ignore you. You can be our eyes and ears."

She offered a faint smile. "And how will I get the information to you?"

"I've learned a few things about hiding in the shadows. Also, I have money, and I expect you to take it."

"I don't like taking your money, but I can do what you ask—and I can keep an eye on Chris and Sheriff Reynolds. I shall surprise you and not complain." Hope crested in her blue eyes.

He peered up at Jed, the man who knew him better than his own father. "You said Governor Eaton was sending a man?"

"Should be here in two days. Name's Dixon. He'll stop at the ranch first."

"Best you send Les off until he's gone. And once Dixon heads for Earnest, stay clear of him where others might see."

"What are you thinking, son?" Jed asked.

Caleb smiled then held his breath sharply as Naomi tightened the bandage. "Another shipment of money en route to

Denver, or at least let the sheriff believe money is on the stage. Chris is angry, and the only way to soothe him will be to satisfy his greed. The sheriff was told that the governor would send an escort on the next shipment, but I think Dixon could persuade him otherwise, especially if an empty strongbox is with the stage. When Chris robs it, Dixon and I will be there. It sounds simple, but I believe it has merit."

"It does," Jed said. "You have a fine plan."

Caleb looked at his bandaged shoulder. It hurt powerful bad. He took a deep breath. "Jed, would you commit the plan to God? We all need prayer."

&

Audra believed she'd not rest a wink that night. So much had happened this evening. The nightmare with Christopher stayed vivid in her mind. Caleb had nearly been killed. The struggle for the revolver and the discovery he'd been injured played back through her thoughts. Tonight he'd spoken the truth; running from the law was no life at all.

She shuddered as she crawled beneath the quilt at Jed and Naomi's. She had not tried to talk to Caleb privately; it would be too difficult for both of them. Her love could strengthen him or weaken him, and she was determined not to be demanding. Later, they'd have hours to talk, to hold each other. It was enough to know he loved her, and he knew she loved him.

She laid her head upon the pillow. An image of Caleb stayed fixed in her mind—a home, a family, a life of peace. She inhaled deeply as sleep nibbled at her body. Living in Earnest alone without her friends could not be worse than sharing meals and worrisome hours with Christopher. Already she sensed his treachery. He'd talk badly about her to his congregation to make sure no one befriended her. In the darkness, she smiled despite the ugliness of tonight and the days to come. Jesus would be her only friend. She'd not be lonely, and she'd not disappoint Him.

seventeen

Caleb saw Jed swing a lantern twice in front of the kitchen window to signal that Dixon had arrived. With Les sent to round up strays for a few days, Caleb felt safer in approaching the Masters' ranch. Governor Eaton must have believed some of what Jed claimed, or he wouldn't have sent Dixon to look into the situation—unless Chris had done the same thing. That being the case, Dixon may have orders to arrest the infamous outlaw. A queasy sensation settled in the pit of Caleb's stomach. With his shoulder healing, he had doubts about his ability to fight his way out of this one.

Rely on God. Caleb took a deep breath.

He waited nearly an hour before he knocked on the door. Uneasiness crept over him; his mouth tasted as dry as an August day without rain. He felt powerless over this stranger who could very well decide his future. The past four years had left him suspicious and afraid to trust anyone. Jed and Naomi smothered him in kindness before he opened up his heart to them. Now they were knee-deep in this mess with him. Shaking his head to dispel the doubts, he knocked on the door.

God possessed the power, not the governor's assigned man or Caleb's ability to fight.

Jed greeted him with a wide grin. "We've been talking about the situation." He ushered Caleb inside. "Dixon is anxious to meet you."

The stranger rose from a chair—tall, thin, confident. Caleb hid his trepidation and gripped the man's hand. "Caleb Windsor here. Pleased to make your acquaintance."

"Just call me Dixon."

The two men locked gazes. *Good eye contact. Tanned face.*

138

Callused hands. Not afraid of work.

"Jed says the wrong man is on the wanted posters." Dixon neither smiled nor moved a muscle. "I need proof."

Caleb paused. "Are you ready to work?"

"Depends on your story," Dixon said.

"Sit down, and I'll give it to you." For the next hour, Caleb told what had happened over the past four years since he and Chris moved to Earnest. All the while he scrutinized the man before him. Dixon's body remained motionless: no tugging at his beard as if doubtful of Caleb's story or lifting of his brow. Intelligence radiated from his eyes.

"Like I said before, we need evidence," Dixon said. "The Masterses' testimony is good, so is Miss Lenders's, but Sheriff Reynolds already filed a report to the governor naming the Masters as part of the gang."

"I'm not surprised. He has one of his men working here for Jed. We need to find out where he stashed the money and the other stolen goods," Caleb said. "I have a plan."

Dixon nodded. "Go on. I'm listening."

"Chris is greedy, and now he's after revenge because of Audra. If the sheriff learns of a money shipment heading to Denver and tells Chris, he'll have to steal it. We don't need the evidence for you to arrest him as long as you catch him during the robbery. I'd even like to see your men as passengers."

"This will go hard on whoever is convicted. Brothers, huh?"

"Yep. Our father's still alive, and I don't want to think about him finding out about this." Caleb paused. "I'm hoping my brother would tell you where the money is in exchange for a lesser sentence."

"Good thinking." Dixon leaned back in his chair. "Give me more details."

Caleb continued, just as he had outlined the plan on the night Chris shot him.

"This is worth a try." Dixon pointed to Caleb's shoulder. "Who winged you?"

"My brother."

"An accident?"

"Nope. The only accident was he missed my heart."

Dixon pressed his lips together. "How long before you can ride and shoot?"

"Tomorrow. Don't fret over me. I'll hold my own."

For the first time, Dixon smiled. "I'm ready to go to work. This will take time."

&

In the wee hours of the morning, long after Caleb rode with Dixon to the outskirts of town then back to the Masters' ranch, he took out paper, pen, and ink from Naomi's kitchen. He remembered where she kept it from the last letter he wrote. That one was for Chris to copy and send to his father about requesting a wife. This time, things were different. He'd be a fool not to comprehend that he or Chris faced possible death over this mess. Caleb's conscience refused to allow their father to believe the years of lies. By candlelight, he dipped the pen into the inkwell and began the painful truth to his father.

> Dear Father,
>
> I should have written to you long before this, but I didn't know where to begin. I still don't. Shame and guilt have eaten away at me for a long time. I pray God guides my pen, and the accountings I relate will not turn you against me or Chris, for it is out of love for you and my brother that I tell you these things.
>
> As boys, it seemed like Chris and I were always in trouble, as you well remember. I hated seeing my brother punished, so I confessed to many things that I didn't do. Over the years, the practice became a habit until Chris expected me to take the blame. I thought taking care of him was a sign of strength, but I was wrong. So wrong. When we moved to Colorado, I thought his behavior would change. I was wrong. Chris met up with some fellows who had no

respect for the law. They became his friends. With them, he found a way to have more horses. I don't think he set out to be an outlaw or to blame me. Their ways were just easier for him to get the things he wanted. When someone recognized him during a raid on a man's farm, he claimed I was the thief. I think out of habit. Soon afterwards he went into the ministry.

Father, I wrote the letter for Chris requesting a wife, and he did not balk at the idea. I thought if my brother married a godly woman, he'd end his life of crime. I didn't mind leaving the country if it brought about good for my brother.

Audra learned the truth about Chris, and she is living at the boardinghouse in Earnest. Audra and a dear couple, Jed and Naomi Masters, are the only ones who know the truth. Wanted posters with my name are nailed in every town in the area. Chris refuses to stop. I am asking you to come to Earnest and help me convince him to end his ways.

I'm sorry for lying to you all these years, and I understand this is my fault. If I had allowed him to face the consequences of his actions all these years, the situation would not have gotten so bad. I need you, Father. I firmly believe he will listen to you. My prayer is for Chris to see he is not pleasing God. Please send your response to the Masters. It is no longer safe for me to be seen.

Your son,
Caleb

For the next few days, Caleb watched Chris every moment of the day until the sun went down. Even then he kept a wary eye on the road leading out of town. He used a pair of binoculars from Jed's Civil War years. If his brother left town, Caleb followed. He observed the company he kept and noted the hours in the parsonage. Only God knew why no one caught him spying.

Chris spent a lot of time in Sheriff Reynolds's office. Most likely discussing what they intended to do with the stolen money. One thought amazed Caleb: How could the sheriff trust Chris with the money, unless he also knew where it was hidden?

Dixon stayed at the boardinghouse, and Caleb felt certain he made contact with Audra. Poor girl, she needed a friend.

Everything rested on finding the money. Caleb had no intentions of giving up. Not this time. Too many people had been robbed of peace, and a life with Audra weighed in the balance.

≥a

If Audra had had any doubt about Christopher's vindictiveness, she had none now. From the way the members of his congregation snubbed her, he must have announced her unwillingness to marry him from the pulpit. The reason must have been scandalous. A pair of ladies from the choir saw her and crossed the street.

"Good afternoon, ladies." Audra bit back her laughter. "Beautiful day, isn't it?"

They kept right on walking.

Sheriff Reynolds treated her like a stranger, but that was a blessing. The man made her want to horsewhip him. Christopher had not set foot inside the boardinghouse lately. Finally she could enjoy her meals, and the tasteless food now had flavor. Finding work was another matter. The idea of Caleb giving her money didn't sit well. Twice she'd talked to the boardinghouse owner and the gentleman who owned the general store, but they had nothing to offer. She approached the head of the school board, but he was a member of Chris's church and stated the town had an excellent teacher. This morning she'd already been to the general store again, the newspaper office, and the livery—the latter had advertised for a stable boy.

The owner, a huge man who more closely resembled a bear, stared at her in surprise. "What does a fine young woman want with a job pitching straw and tending to horses?"

"I need to pay for my room and board," she said. "I can do

this." The thought suddenly occurred to her that she could keep her eyes on Christopher by working there. "Sir, I'm a hard worker. I can be here early and stay late."

He crossed his arms across his barreled chest and teetered back on his heels. "As pretty as you are, I don't want all the young men of Earnest filling up my livery."

"Absolutely not," she said. "I'd be here to work."

He nodded. "All right. I need you in the morning at six—and you best be stopping by the general store and finding yourself some suitable clothes. Can't clean out stalls with a skirt trailing in the manure."

"I will, sir. And thank you very much."

The owner's last instruction would take about half the money she had left, but she now had a job to support herself. *Christopher, you can't come and go without me knowing it. Thank You, Lord. This job is truly a gift from You.*

At the general store, she purchased a pair of boy's overalls, a shirt, boots, and two pairs of socks. A hat crossed her mind, until she remembered she'd be inside the livery and the sun wouldn't touch her face. Good thing Mama and Papa weren't nearby to see her mode of dress. She hoped Caleb didn't change his mind about her once he saw her knee-deep in dirty straw.

On the second day of her employ, a stranger walked into the livery and asked for his horse. Audra knew the animal, a high-spirited stallion that left her shaking in her boots.

"I'll give you a hand," the man said. "Are you the only one working today?"

Audra nodded. Suddenly a pang of fear crept through her. After all she was a woman alone in a livery stable. "Yes, sir." In the faint light, he looked very large. Almost as big as the livery owner.

"Can we talk in private, Miss Lenders?"

He knew her name. "What about?"

"Your friends. My name is Dixon—sent by Governor Eaton."

She relaxed with that knowledge. "Are they all right?"

"One of them would like to see you this evening. I could come by the boardinghouse and escort you in a wagon. I'm staying there, too, so I'm hoping this looks like we're courting." He smiled. "As pretty as you are, I can see why Caleb is a little anxious."

She blushed. "I am, too."

He glanced about. "Quite smart of you to obtain employment here."

"Thank you. It's been only a few days, but Christopher can't leave town without me knowing it."

"Caleb and I are following him, too. Although he could have conversations here that only you'd be privy to."

"I want to do whatever I can."

"Be careful. If what I've heard is true, Christopher Windsor is a dangerous man."

She nodded.

"All right, Miss Lenders. My horse can be a handful, so I'll saddle him up."

"Thank you. He's fed and groomed."

He chuckled. "Do you always keep company with outlaws and unruly horses?"

She smiled at the thought. *My adventure.* "Goodness, it looks that way."

Mr. Dixon continued to laugh all the while he was in the livery. When he left, her day flew by. All she could think about was seeing Caleb. And he wanted to see her.

Not too long after the noon hour, Christopher came by for his horse and wagon. "What are you doing here?"

"Working," she said.

He sneered. "Too bad I didn't talk to the owner first."

"Must you be so spiteful?" she asked. "Why would you want a woman who loves another man?"

"An outlaw? I'm not stupid, Audra. You've been seeing my brother since the stage holdup."

Her stomach churned. Had Christopher convinced himself

of his innocence? "I know who you are, and I know what you've done."

He shook his head while lines deepened across his brow. "I could have given you anything you wanted. Instead you betrayed me."

She shivered. Perhaps he *had* cared for her—in the only way he knew. She doubted if he understood the real meaning of love when he had no respect for God.

"I'll get your horse and wagon ready." She turned toward the stalls.

"No, thanks. I'll handle it myself. I can't trust you any more than I can Caleb."

Evening shadows lingered by the time Mr. Dixon called on her. Excitement raced through her veins at the thought of seeing Caleb. She hoped his shoulder had healed nicely. Oh, for the day when he didn't have to hide out like a criminal.

"You look quite lovely, Miss Lenders," Mr. Dixon said. "I have a daughter your age, and the both of you could rival the queens of Europe."

"Thank you. I should like to meet her."

"A pleasant thought, especially if you and your friend can travel about freely." They walked through the door and on to the awaiting wagon. He assisted her onto the seat. "We may be followed, so be prepared if you're not able to see him," he whispered.

The thought devastated her, but she understood. A sideways glance took in Christopher and the sheriff observing them from across the street. "Certainly, Mr. Dixon," she said with a smile. "This is a pleasant evening for a ride."

Once they traveled north outside of town, Audra sought conversation to soothe her uneasiness. "I'm glad we're headed opposite of the Masterses' ranch. Perhaps Christopher and the sheriff will think we aren't worth the trouble."

"I'd like to agree with you but, until Caleb rides into view, we'll continue alone."

For the next hour while dusk rested night upon them,

Audra and Dixon ambled north. At one point, he stopped to light the kerosene lanterns on both sides. A short while later, he reined in the horse and gestured for her not to speak. The sound of approaching riders met their ears.

"Don't be afraid," he said. "I'm armed, and Caleb is watching." He turned the wagon around as the riders grew nearer. "Hello there," he said. "Who goes there?"

"Sheriff Reynolds and Pastor Windsor."

Audra recognized the sheriff's voice. Now what excuse would they use?

"Is there a problem?" Mr. Dixon asked. By then the two riders came into view and stopped in front of the wagon.

"We were checking on a rumor that Miss Lenders may be in danger." The sheriff cleared his throat. "We've had some problems with a local outlaw and didn't want either of you to face him alone. He's already killed one man and robbed a good many folk."

"Thank you. Appreciate your concern. We haven't had any trouble, and we're on our way back to town." Confidence radiated from Mr. Dixon's voice.

"Miss Lenders, would you like an escort?" the sheriff asked. "Pastor here was concerned."

She stiffened. "I'm fine. We haven't seen anyone to alarm us."

"We're just looking out for our citizens." Sheriff Reynolds tipped his hat.

Mr. Dixon picked up his reins and urged the horse on. A tear slipped down Audra's cheek. She'd wanted to see Caleb. Silence prevailed until they reached Earnest.

"I'm sorry," Mr. Dixon said. "Those two don't trust a move you make—possibly mine, too. The sheriff could have learned who I am."

"You've gone to a great deal of trouble tonight. I can take care of the horse and wagon."

"I think not, Miss Lenders, but to continue our little ruse, you may accompany me to the livery."

The livery was deserted, but Mr. Dixon had already made

arrangements to return the horse and wagon late. Audra waited while he unhitched the wagon then led the horse into the stable.

A man stepped from the shadows. She held her breath. Had Christopher or the sheriff decided to do them harm?

eighteen

"Audra," Caleb whispered to the slight figure before him. "It's all right." He moved closer and cast aside his resolve not to reveal the intensity of his feelings for her. She looked incredibly small standing there with only the faint light of the lantern coming from the rear of the stable. The halo outlining her body gave her an angelic effect. He pulled her from the entrance back into the blackness and held her close. At first she trembled, but in the next breath she relaxed in his arms. He smelled the faint scent of flowers about her, and his knees weakened. A fierce protective nature seized him.

"I shouldn't be doing this," he said. "Later I'll apologize."

"No, don't. Here in your arms is where I want to be."

"This is where you belong." Perhaps the darkness gave him courage to speak his heart—or made him foolhardy. "I shouldn't be saying this either. I've come for you, Audra."

"What do you mean? Where are we going? Mexico? Canada?"

"Neither of those. I'm taking you to Jed and Naomi. It's not safe here. I've watched Chris and the sheriff follow you. I'm not having you in danger any longer," Caleb said.

She wrapped her arms around his chest. "I thought you wanted me in Earnest."

"I'm afraid he'll hurt you, blame it on me."

She sighed, and he sensed her rebellious streak taking over. "I'm not afraid. My job here at the livery affords me the chance to watch him and the sheriff. Christopher wouldn't dare hurt me and discredit his reputation."

"Evenin', Caleb," Dixon said. Caleb hadn't heard him approach. "In my opinion she's in more danger at the Masterses' place. Listen to me for a moment. He could ride in there and shoot the three of them and cover for it just like he's covered everything else. And you know who'd be held responsible."

Caleb had considered the same, but he could keep a better eye out for them at the ranch.

"If he shot you, don't you think he'd do the same to your friends?" Dixon asked.

"Caleb, please. He's right." Audra stepped back, and he grasped her hand. "I'm safer here. He's been avoiding me until tonight."

"Don't think either of them knows why I'm staying in Earnest," Dixon said. "I prefer not telling them for as long as possible. If he's as suspicious as he appeared tonight, he'll be after me soon. The diversion might cause him to do something stupid—and that's what I need."

"Could buy time," Caleb said. Every day that passed increased the chances of finding the money, but he still believed Audra was safer with the Masterses. "I'd hoped to find what we needed without letting him believe another shipment of money was on its way." *I don't want my brother killed in all of this, only stopped.*

"You have too much on your mind," Dixon said. "Let's head out of here. Did you say your father was coming?"

Audra gasped. "Pastor Windsor is coming to Earnest?"

"I wrote him, asked him to help me with Chris," Caleb said.

"Do you think he will?" Audra asked.

"Possibly. The letter was a confession about what had been going on. Depends if he believed me or not."

Audra turned to him. "Oh, if he could convince—"

Caleb squeezed her hand. He heard voices, and at this late hour that could only mean trouble. In the time it took to breathe in and out, the voices mingled outside the livery.

"What do you think those two were up to?" Chris asked.

"Meetin' up with your brother," Sheriff Reynolds said. "Dixon works for the governor, and he's taken up with Miss Lenders. I'm not stupid. They're working together."

"Dixon believes Caleb?" Chris asked.

"I'm saying he's stuck his nose into our business. I'm going to talk to him tomorrow. Ask him if he's found Caleb, like I've known all along who he is."

"Doesn't matter 'cause they don't have any evidence," Chris said. "I'm going home. Had enough for one day."

"You frettin' about Les, too?"

"I'll take care of him. He's gotten greedy. You handle Dixon."

※

Later Audra recalled every sight and sound of the evening. What started out as a hopeful few stolen moments with Caleb turned into a game of deception. No longer did she doubt that Christopher would hurt her. She believed he'd do anything to save himself—reminding her of Caleb's story of when the two boys played too close to the water's edge.

She prayed Pastor Windsor came to Earnest. This was hope, the possibility of Christopher confessing to what he'd done. But that meant weeks more when she inwardly begged for this to be over now.

Two weeks passed and then a third. Audra watched her once-wedding day come and go. She felt bad about missing church on Wednesday nights and Sundays, but she used those hours to read through the Old Testament. Her days at the livery left her exhausted, and Christopher stayed close to town. Perhaps the chance to catch him with the money had passed.

Not once did she see Caleb; she believed the threat of being caught kept him away. That was like him, staying clear to protect her and the Masters. Many times she wondered how Dixon and the others planned to ensnare Christopher, and her patience wore thin.

The wife of the boardinghouse owner had started to say hello once in a while, but nothing else. Audra felt like a soiled dove, not good enough to hold a conversation with respectable folks. Dixon, her sole source of communication from Naomi, Jed, and Caleb, often left town early in the morning and didn't return until after she finished at the livery.

One warm afternoon, she recognized Jed's voice asking for her from the livery owner.

"Miss Audra, a couple of gentlemen here to see you." Annoyance rang through his voice.

She stuck her pitchfork into a wet, nasty pile of straw and hurried to the front. Jed caught her attention immediately, but she had to blink a few times in order to see the other man. Her pulse raced with the recognition.

"Audra," a booming voice said.

"Pastor Windsor." She longed to hug him as she used to in Nebraska, but the scent of horses and what she'd been cleaning clung to her.

"Where's my hug?" he asked.

She shook her head. "I smell terrible. But it is so good to see you."

"I don't care a lick. You're like a daughter to me."

She wrapped her arms around his thin waist then stepped back. She smelled so bad she couldn't stand herself.

Not knowing who might be listening, she picked through her words. "What brings you to Earnest? Christopher and I did not marry."

"I got word of the news. Right now, I have a few things to clear up." His face dimmed. "Audra, I'm so sorry to have sent you out here to this unfortunate situation." The lines in his face deepened.

"None of this is your fault. I'm sure you're the man to help right things. I feel better knowing you are here."

"Jed is allowing me to stay with him and his wife for a few days. I have to find out the truth."

"I had to learn the hard way," she said.

His face clouded even more than before. It seemed as though he might weep. " 'Tis a sad day when a father is deceived. For many years I thought I understood my sons. Now it appears I've been wrong."

"Do my parents know you are here?"

"I left word with an elder to ride out to their place. I headed here as soon as I received the letter."

"Miss Audra," the livery owner said. "You have work to do."

She glanced at Jed and gave him a big smile. "The situation will be remedied soon. You'll see."

"We're paying a visit at the parsonage before heading to the ranch," Jed said. "We could use a little prayer."

Audra wished them well and rushed back to her task of cleaning out stalls. She shivered, and her stomach churned with what Pastor Windsor needed to do. What if Christopher convinced him that Caleb was the outlaw? But the pastor had come all this way, and for that she was happy and relieved.

❧

Caleb watched the sun crest the horizon. He'd expected his father and Jed over an hour ago. Doubts crept over him. If only he could have heard the conversation going on between Chris and his father. At the very least, he'd liked to have defended himself. At least Jed was there. The thought of his father making the journey to Earnest amazed him. When Jed said he'd received a wire from Nebraska confirming his father's journey to Colorado, Caleb had difficulty believing it. They hadn't really talked in years since he was always in trouble, or so it appeared.

In his solitary position overlooking the Masterses' ranch, Caleb saw smoke rise from the chimney and visualized Naomi cooking supper. He smiled, thinking how she'd been as close to a mother as he'd ever find. And Jed, well, as he'd thought before, the man knew him better than his own father. Caleb wished it all could change among the Windsor men, but the bad communication had been his fault. He understood his failings now, whereas before he believed he'd acted out of love.

As the last bit of sunlight slipped behind the mountains, Caleb's gaze rested on the road leading from Earnest. Jed drove the wagon with Father seated alongside him. He headed toward them. Caleb's heart pounded. He felt like a kid again, afraid of what his father would say about his latest bout of mischief.

"Evenin', Father, Jed." Caleb's horse moved into their path.

Jed stopped the wagon, but Caleb barely noticed. His gaze was fixed on his father, although he couldn't see his face clearly in the near darkness.

"Caleb, it's been a long time." The deep voice resounded around him. How many times had that voice scared him to death? The man had used a switch on Caleb more than a few times—after he'd confessed to something Chris had done.

"Yes, sir. Thank you. I appreciate your coming."

"Son, we have a lot of catching up to do."

Caleb swallowed a lump in his throat. He fought to gain his composure. "I'm sorry about the circumstances bringing you here."

"Caleb, you never asked me for a thing in your life. I'd have traveled across both oceans, if you'd requested it." His voice broke, leaving Caleb longing to wrap his arms around his father's neck. But he couldn't move a muscle to dismount. He was supposed to be a man, not a kid running to Papa for help. "Are you coming with Jed and me?" his father asked.

"Not till later when the ranch hands have turned in."

"I see. I'll be spending a few days with these kind folk."

"Good. I'd like to show you what I can of my own ranch."

"I'd like that. I'd like that very much."

nineteen

Once Caleb noted that Les had not come from the bunk-house for the past several minutes, he made his way to the Masterses' door. He'd spent the past two hours mulling over what to say to his father in such a way that Chris appeared less a criminal. Of course, he'd spent most of his life making his brother look good.

Jed must have heard his boots on the front porch for he opened the door and gestured him inside. As usual Naomi had prepared a feast with plenty left over for him.

"Glad to hear you take good care of my boy," his father said to Naomi. "My cooking liked to starve my boys to death. And they had little affection from women."

Caleb met his gaze—no malice, no accusations. In the past, Father spoke the words while he listened. *How does a grown man discuss his brother's rebellious behavior with their father?*

"I saw Christopher today," his father said. "Naomi, may I trouble you for another cup of your fine coffee."

She beamed. "Of course. How about a sugar cookie to go with it?"

"Those are my favorite," he said. "What about you, son?"

"Uh, no, thanks." The time to visit grew near. He shook in his boots.

Naomi set the coffee and cookie before Caleb's father. "Jed and I are heading to bed. Pastor, we'll see you in the morning. Caleb, be safe." She kissed his cheek.

Jed scooted his chair back from the braid rug and grabbed a cookie and his mug of coffee. "Caleb, this is what you've prayed for. Let God handle the reins."

Caleb nodded and bid them good night. Once the couple closed their bedroom door, he fought for the appropriate words. *God help me.* "I don't know how to begin."

"We let too many silent years pass between us."

"I agree." Suddenly Caleb's coffee tasted bitter. "But it was my fault."

"No, son. I was too busy doing God's work to do anything about the deceit in my own family."

Caleb blinked. "I don't understand."

"I knew you couldn't have done all the things you admitted to, but I left the matter alone. It was easier for me to discipline you than find out why you took the blame. I owe you an apology. I've sought God's forgiveness. Will you forgive me?"

Startled, Caleb allowed his father's words to wash over him. "Yes, sir. I never had any idea that you knew I wasn't at fault."

"I wondered why, but I neglected to seek out the answers. On the way out here, I had plenty of time to reflect on the years you and Christopher were boys. I realized Christopher never had anything good to say about you, and you never had anything bad to say about him. I despise myself for not seeing through what was going on."

Caleb had always sensed the deep responsibility his father possessed in raising his sons and serving God's people. "You had so much work—"

His father waved his hand. "That's not an excuse." He took a deep breath, and for a moment Caleb feared the man would weep. "Would you like to hear about my meeting with Christopher?"

"Very much."

"He was surprised and more than a little upset with me for not writing him about my arrival. He showed me his church and invited me and Jed inside the parsonage. Jed elected to take a walk, leaving us alone. First I asked him about Audra, and he said she'd not proven to be a fit choice for a wife."

Anger simmered in Caleb. "How did you respond?"

"I told him Audra Lenders was a fine young woman, and I didn't appreciate him slandering her fine reputation. Then I asked him about you. He'd written some time ago about your unlawful activities and how you'd damaged his ministry. He said he hated to break the news to me, but you were wanted for murder and robbery. He said you had corrupted Audra and led her astray. He also told me to beware of the Masterses. The law suspected them of hiding you."

Caleb listened to every word. "I swear to you, Father, I have never robbed anyone and never killed a man. Pull out your Bible, and I will swear on the Word of God. I know I shouldn't have said that. My word should be enough." He took a deep breath. "My guilt is covering up for Chris, because now one of us will end up behind bars."

"I don't want to believe either of my sons is capable of murder, but if one is to be punished, I pray it is the guilty one. I told him about your letter and said I was here to learn the truth."

Caleb startled. "You told him about the letter?"

His father nodded. "He called you a liar. I asked him if his words were those of a man of God. He told me to seek out the truth."

"I'd do anything to spare you this heartache," Caleb said. "I'm not expecting you to take sides or choose who is telling the truth tonight. But I am asking you to search for God's wisdom in this, and I promise your decision will never sway the love I have for you."

His father's eyes moistened. "What more could I ask? For now—"

The sound of horses alerted Caleb. He rose to the window and pulled aside the curtain just far enough to view the commotion. "It's Chris and the sheriff."

"They're after you?"

"Yeah, and I need to get out of here."

Jed opened the bedroom door. He was still fully dressed as though he suspected what might happen. "This way, Caleb."

Without hesitation or a glance his father's way, Caleb stepped into the bedroom. Naomi stood with their window open. How miserable for his father to see him running from his own brother like an outlaw.

He climbed through an open window into the warm night air. He heard the sheriff and Chris on the front porch right around the corner from him.

"Evenin', Jed," Sheriff Reynolds said. "We got wind that Caleb was in these parts. Thought we'd stop in and make sure you folks were all right. The pastor here is concerned about his father."

"Thanks, Sheriff. Come on in and sit a spell," Jed said. "We're fine, just talking."

"Go ahead Christopher," the sheriff said. "I'll take a look out here and check with the hands to see if they've seen anything suspicious."

Caleb lit out into the night. If not for his father and Audra, he'd strongly consider riding toward Mexico.

"Caleb."

He whirled around toward the familiar voice near the shed. "Dixon?"

"Yeah. Been watching the house and couldn't get to you fast enough."

Caleb hurried to him. "Those two don't trust anyone, do they?"

Dixon chuckled. "Would you with thousands of dollars at stake?"

"That much?"

"You bet," Dixon said. "If you figure the cattle and horses stolen, gold watches and jewelry and money, it could be even more."

The two ducked behind trees and sheds until they were clear of the house. Dixon had left his horse tied next to Caleb's.

"When can we get the word out about a money shipment to Denver?" Caleb asked. "I've lost my patience with Chris."

"Tomorrow I'll ride to Denver and set it up with the governor. Then I'll make sure the sheriff finds out. Let's hope they take the bait."

"Pray." Caleb said. "I'm afraid this will be my last chance to prove my innocence."

❧

Audra questioned the fact Dixon left Earnest the day after Pastor Windsor arrived. It had been over three days, and still he hadn't returned. She'd grown to depend on him to keep her informed of what happened with Caleb. She remembered when she gave herself four weeks to find the evidence against Christopher. What a foolish idea, thinking a time restraint would aid her. Only God understood her need to help clear Caleb's name.

Like a crack of thunder in the middle of the night, realization took form and seized her senses. All this time, she'd asked God to go with her instead of depending on Him to lead the way. Oh, she'd gone through the ritual of pleading for guidance and deliverance, but when things failed to work out like she wanted, she took it upon herself to take over.

God, I'm so sorry. Everything with Caleb is frightening, and I don't know what to do. Now I see I've been attempting to lead instead of follow You. I thought if I gave myself a limited amount of time to get information from Christopher, You would oblige me. How horribly wrong I've been. From this moment on, I will seek You with my whole heart. I'm trusting You to save Caleb from those who wish to do him harm. I pray Christopher repents of his sins as well as the others who ride with him. Forgive me, God.

She stuck the pitchfork into fresh hay. *And, God, help Caleb unite with his father.*

"Audra," the livery owner said. "Pastor Windsor and Sheriff Reynolds need their horses."

Follow them, a voice said. *Leave the livery and go. You don't need this job.*

❧

Caleb gestured to the west of where he and his father rode. Lush, variegated green circled his ranch on three sides with a valley of thick pastures for his cattle and horses.

"Beautiful land, son. No wonder you're proud of it."

"Yes, sir. We've added plenty of calves and foals this spring."

"How long since you've been able to live there?" His father's voice rang with sadness.

"About a year. My foreman's a good man. I moved him and his family into my house until this is over."

"What are your plans?"

Caleb studied him. It seemed as though his father believed him, but he didn't want to ask. The past few days with Father had been memorable, no matter what happened. "Not sure. I have my dreams like most men."

"Do they include Audra Lenders?"

Dare he confess his love for her? "I think that dream would come as close to heaven as I could get."

"I want your dreams to be your future." His father sighed. "Christopher has not asked me to stay with him or inquired as to how long I plan to stay."

Caleb thought better of replying. He could see the grief in his father's eyes.

"Is that because he plans to leave the country?" his father continued. When Caleb still didn't respond he stared into the valley. "This grieves us both, and I am helpless to convince him otherwise. How sad it is to know your own son has deceived those he claims to shepherd."

"God will see us through this," Caleb said.

Silence, save for the calls of a crow, surrounded them. Welcoming a diversion, Caleb pointed to a couple of frisky colts racing like the wind. They both laughed.

"What are Dixon's plans?"

"Father, it will grieve you."

His father shook his head. "I'm a grown man. How does Audra feel when you refuse to tell her things?"

Caleb lifted his hat. "I think you know the answer." He chuckled in remembering her independent nature. "She is a stubborn one, but I like her spunk—as long as she doesn't get hurt."

"Is she in the safest place?"

"Since I've done everything but carry her to the stage, I guess so. I used to think living with Jed and Naomi was the best, but Dixon feared Chris might—"

"No need to finish."

"Thanks. I do love her. God has kept me steady company for a long time, and He's given me a glimpse of a woman's love."

"After your mother, I didn't want any other woman."

Caleb understood. "Audra reminds you of her, doesn't she?"

"Not in looks, but in spirit." His father laughed. "You are in for an exciting life."

"I hope so."

"Now tell me what Dixon has planned," his father said.

Caleb hesitated then told him every word. If he couldn't trust his father, who could he trust? "The stage is scheduled to arrive tomorrow late morning."

"Are you seeing Audra tonight?"

"No, I can't. If things go bad, well, it's better this way."

ঽ

Audra stretched her back and shoulder muscles. She ached all over. Not sleeping had a lot to do with it. Her body craved rest, but when she lay down, her mind spun with thoughts of Caleb. She had no idea what he and Dixon planned or how Pastor Windsor, Jed, and Naomi fared during this.

Trust God. The thought stayed foremost in her mind. She remembered the afternoon she felt the urge to leave the livery and trail after Christopher and the sheriff. She realized the insistence did not come from God, and she willed the voice away. Since then, she continued to pray, although it proved to be the hardest thing she'd ever done.

She walked from the livery, a bit later than usual and headed to the boardinghouse. The owner complained about her ordering a bath every evening, but just because she worked cleaning out horse stables didn't mean she had to smell like one. Her stomach growled. Naomi's cooking sure sounded better than the boardinghouse's.

After her bath, she followed her nose to the dining room. This was chicken soup and corn bread night. Right now it didn't matter what she ate, anything to fill her stomach.

"Miss Lenders."

Audra turned to face Sheriff Reynolds. "Good evening, sir."

"I hate to tell you this, but there's been some trouble."

Her stomach twisted. "What happened?"

"Shooting at the Masterses' place, Miss Lenders." He removed his hat. "I'm real sorry."

"Who's been hurt?" Her voice quivered. Her hands trembled.

"Jed didn't make it." He took a deep breath. "Caleb is hurt bad. He's asking for you."

twenty

"Shall we take the wagon or ride to the Masterses' ranch?" Sheriff Reynolds asked Audra.

"The horses are faster." She bit back a sob. All along she understood one of the Windsor twins would be hurt, but she wasn't ready to face it. "Is Christopher hurt?"

"He's tending to his brother. Blood is thicker than the outlaw life."

Oh, God, You can right this. You can comfort Naomi. You can heal Caleb's body. "What about the doctor?"

"He's not home, out on a call."

Once the horses were saddled, she spurred hers toward the Masterses' ranch.

"Slow down, Miss Lenders," the sheriff said.

She matched her mare's pace to his. Confusion etched her mind. They were on a dark road far from town and far from Jed and Naomi's. Another rider joined them, but in the blackness she couldn't tell who he was.

"What is going on?" she asked.

"A trade."

Audra froze at the sound of the voice. "Christopher," she whispered. "I thought you were with Caleb."

He laughed. "You mean my poor wounded brother? I might miss my target once, but not twice. I have no idea where he is. Probably running for the hills."

"And Jed?"

"Most likely sleeping or eating." Christopher laughed.

"You tricked me." Her gaze flew to the sheriff. "You lied to me."

"Afraid so," the sheriff said.

"Why? What do you want me for?"

162

Christopher laughed again. "You and I, sweet lady, are heading to Mexico."

Was he crazy? "I will not."

"You have no choice. Once we're safe inside the border, you can do whatever you want," Christopher said. "This is your fault. I'd have treated you fine in Mexico, if you hadn't betrayed me with Caleb."

Her heart pounded. "You won't get away with this. Too many people are wise to your treachery."

"Not enough people who amount to anything." Christopher's low, sneering voice shook her resolve.

"A stage is headed this way tomorrow with a sizeable amount of money," the sheriff said. "We're taking it off the driver's hands, and you are our protection. Nobody is going to bother us as long as we have you hostage."

Audra gasped.

"See, we got wind of what Dixon and Caleb planned. Doesn't do them a bit of good to try to catch us robbing the stage when we have you," Christopher said.

"Caleb will come after me." Audra attempted to sound strong.

"Watch us," Christopher said and snatched up her reins. "Tonight you're staying with me, and tomorrow you're going to ride with us."

They broke from the road, and the horses picked their way over a rough path. They made so many twists and turns that she soon became lost. Her comfort rested in God. He knew exactly where she rode with the sheriff and Christopher.

How could Caleb find the evidence they needed when Christopher held her hostage? The situation looked incredibly desperate. Without God's intervention, Christopher once again triumphed.

"Where's the money?" the sheriff asked Christopher.

"In a safe place."

"You don't have it with you?"

"I have everything worked out," Christopher spat at the

sheriff like a mad cat.

The sheriff cursed. "You left it all at the parsonage?"

"Think about it. A guilty pastor would not show his face in town. An innocent man returns to his work. I'll get it after we hold up the stage."

"Reckon you make sense," Sheriff Reynolds said. "I'll keep an eye on Miss Audra while you get back to town. Are you sure no one knows about the cave? I don't want Dixon finding me there with her."

"You hadn't been there before, and you've lived here for twenty years."

She clamped her teeth into her lower lip to keep from crying out. Christopher had devised a most clever plan. He admitted storing the stolen money in the parsonage. She could have found it, if not for her stupidity. She could have helped Caleb clear his name. The moment Audra criticized her inability to help the man she loved, she remembered her trust in God. That's all she had left.

ɞ

The next morning, Jed, Dixon, Caleb, and his father watched the approaching stage far enough from the road so as not to alert Christopher and his men. Dixon used binoculars and Caleb stared in the stage's direction. So much rode on what happened today: his innocence, Chris's capture, the heartache of their father, and Audra. If he dwelt on the gravity of it all for very long, he'd not be able to think past the next minute.

"That's not good." Dixon lowered the binoculars then brought them to his eyes again.

"What's going on?" Caleb asked. Had the stage already been stopped? Two of the governor's men rode inside with an empty strongbox. They were armed, but Chris had more men.

Dixon handed him the binoculars. "Take a look for yourself on that far ridge while I figure out what to do." He gestured north of them.

Caleb peered through the lenses. Chris, Sheriff Reynolds, Les, and two other men sat atop their horses. A woman was with them. Gagged. Fury spiked through Caleb. "They have Audra!"

"Christopher believes he's holding an ace," Dixon said.

"What would you call it?" Caleb roared.

"A challenge," Dixon replied.

A rustle in the trees behind them seized their attention. Jim Hawk rode into view. "Gentlemen, you have a problem."

"Let her go," Caleb said. "She has nothing to do with this."

Hawk ignored him and turned to Dixon. "We'll let her go once we get to Mexico. In the meantime, you stay clear of our plans."

"And if we refuse?" Dixon asked.

"Caleb loses his lady." Hawk turned his horse toward the brush and trees. "Consider yourself warned. We've watched every move you've made," he said, just before he disappeared.

"Men, we prayed earlier for God to go before us," his father said. "But I implore you to pause with me and pray for Audra's safety and for victory." Without waiting for a response, his low voice echoed around them. "Oh great and mighty God, protect Audra from those who seek to do her harm. Turn my son's heart to You. Let the evil in my household end today, amen."

"The men inside the stage will be killed if we turn our backs on them," Dixon said. "My guess is only one man will stay behind with Audra."

"I'm going after her," Caleb said. "I can get her out of there before the stage comes by."

Jed shielded his eyes and pointed to the road. "The stage is coming now. You don't have enough time."

"Then stop this whole thing." Caleb sensed the desperation roiling through him.

"Impossible," Dixon said.

"You are sending an innocent woman to her death," Caleb said. "At least your men have guns. Dixon, I've got to go after her." He glanced at his father. "I want my name cleared, but not at the expense of Audra. You will see today what I've claimed. Maybe you can talk some sense into Christopher."

Dixon cleared his throat. "Caleb, it doesn't look good for you to disappear just before the stage is robbed."

"It doesn't matter." Caleb dug his heels into the mare's sides and hurried to the ridge. All he could think about was Audra and setting her free from Chris's men. As much as he hated to believe his brother might harm her, he understood Chris would do whatever it took to protect himself.

For the many months Caleb had been on the run, he'd learned the back trails. His horse stepped over familiar rock and climbed up a narrow path to the ridge. He believed Chris put his faith in his plan, not in the God of the innocent.

Today, there will be one more crime blamed on me. Lord, I don't care if I meet You this very hour, but please let me be there in time for Audra.

Hawk's horse stood beside Audra's mare, close enough that a man could not pass between. The others were gone, meaning he simply had Hawk to deal with. A sense of fear danced up and down his spine, as if he were walking into a trap. Caleb refused to consider the eerie sensation. He had a mission.

Peering in every direction, Caleb saw no one. He rode into the clearing behind Hawk and Audra with his rifle in hand. "Hawk, toss your gun onto the ground," Caleb said.

"You don't listen. I told you what would happen if you tried to interfere with our business."

"Looks to me like you and I are the only ones here," Caleb said, reining in his horse. "Drop the gun."

He heard the click of a revolver. "You never were very smart," Chris said. "I set a trap, and you walked right in."

Audra turned and for a moment Caleb caught her gaze. The end had surely come.

❧

Audra bit back the stinging tears.

"You never had a lick of sense," Christopher said. "Only a fool cares for people the way you do."

"Then I guess I'm a fool. But I'd rather die a good man than live a life like an animal."

"Shall I tell you how this is going to happen?" Christopher asked. "Not that you have a choice in the matter."

"Why not, since I'm the fool?"

"First of all, we're changing clothes. Then I'm putting a bullet right through your heart. Once we're finished with the stage, I'm heading back to Earnest. Dixon will find you with a bullet and think it's me. After all, you left them to come after Audra. Proves you were the one behind this all along. I'll gather up a few things I need then I'm heading to Mexico."

"What about Audra?"

"She's going with me."

Audra wished she could scream. The sound rose and fell in her throat.

"How low have you gone to murder for money?" Caleb asked.

"When I'm living high, I might take the time to contemplate your question."

Pastor Windsor joined them in the clearing. "Christopher, stop this here and now."

Chris paused then stiffened. "I. . .I'm—heading south. You can come along if you like."

"Why would I want to be a part of this? I heard what you plan to do. You'll have to kill your brother *and* your father to get away with this."

Christopher's face clouded. For an instant, remorse etched his features. He shrugged. "Makes no difference to me."

"Yes, it does. You've lived this life long enough to know it leads nowhere. How are you going to sleep? Who will ever trust you? End this today."

"Can't do that." Christopher swung his revolver in Caleb's direction. "Take the shirt off."

Gunfire sounded in the distance, and Audra knew the other men had stopped the stage. Caleb dismounted and unbuttoned his blue chambray shirt. *Help them, God. Turn Christopher's heart.* He tossed it onto the ground. *Dear Jesus, please do something.*

"Why don't we fight it out right here," Caleb said. "Climb down off that horse, coward."

Christopher's face reddened. He threw a bundle of clothes at Caleb's feet. "I don't have time for that. Hawk, wait for me in the trees."

Before Hawk could oblige, Audra kicked her mare, and the horse jumped. A shot whizzed through the air just above Hawk's head. His horse reared, giving Pastor Windsor time to knock Christopher's rifle from his hand. Caleb pulled Hawk from his horse, reached for a rope tied around his saddle, and wrapped it around the big man's hands.

"This is the end of the line." Caleb watched while Pastor Windsor yanked Christopher from his stallion.

Caleb helped Audra from her mare and untied the gag around her mouth. Tears spilled over her cheeks, tears of joy and tears of anguish over the Windsor men.

"It's all over." Caleb pulled her close. "Don't cry"

She snuggled against him and allowed his arms to engulf her. His hands smoothed her hair, causing her to feel like a beloved child.

"Are you hurt?" he asked.

She shook her head. "Just relieved." Her gaze turned to Pastor Windsor. Shock registered across his ashen face at how evil Christopher had become.

"Where's the money?" Pastor Windsor said to Christopher. "It will go easier on you if you tell me." He picked up the rifle.

How sad for the pastor to hold his own son at gunpoint.

"If I can't have it, then no one else will either." Christopher sneered.

"For once do something that is good, and tell me where you hid the money."

Chris's face tightened. He stared at his father.

"Son, whatever happens, I'm here for you. So is Caleb."

Still not a muscle moved in his face.

"Please," Audra said. "Your father and brother will not

desert you. We're all family."

Christopher nodded, and his gaze lingered on her. *He did have feelings for me.* His glance moved to his father again. "I won't hang if I tell you about the money?"

Pastor Windsor pressed his lips together. "I don't know what will happen in a court of law. Your future in this world is up to a judge and jury. My guess is you'll be in prison for a long time."

"Will you visit me?"

Christopher sounded like a small boy—a frightened little child.

"Yes, son."

Christopher took a deep breath. "It's in the small trap door beneath the pulpit."

"Good, now we're going to walk down this ridge and meet Mr. Dixon and his men. Caleb, I have these two where I want them. You go ahead and get Miss Audra back to the Masterses' ranch."

Audra hadn't realized how tightly she'd been clinging to Caleb. He kissed the top of her head. "Come on, sweetheart," he whispered. "Let's go see Naomi. She's probably scared out of her wits."

She nodded. A little while later, the ranch house and buildings came into view.

"Did you mean what you said to Chris?" he asked.

Confused, her mind failed to recall what she'd said. Her body still shook. "I don't remember."

"You said that we're all family."

"And we are." Audra could not deny Christopher as a part of her and Caleb's life any more than she could ignore one of her brothers and sisters.

"So you'll marry me?"

"Today if you want."

Caleb grinned and reached across his horse to take her hand. "The road ahead will be rough with Chris's trial and helping my father endure it all, but I do love you, Audra. I will love and protect you for as long as I live."

"And I will love you forever."

He smiled and nodded. "When we get to the ranch, I'm going to kiss you."

"You mean you're not asking permission?" Audra hid her delight.

"I don't want to give you a chance to say no."

"Mr. Windsor, if I'm going to be Mrs. Windsor, then there needs to be a lot of kisses."

Caleb squeezed her hand lightly and winked. A nudging in her spirit told her a new adventure was about to begin—the biggest adventure of all.

A Letter To Our Readers

Dear Reader:

In order that we might better contribute to your reading enjoyment, we would appreciate your taking a few minutes to respond to the following questions. We welcome your comments and read each form and letter we receive. When completed, please return to the following:

Fiction Editor
Heartsong Presents
PO Box 719
Uhrichsville, Ohio 44683

1. Did you enjoy reading *Renegade Husband* by DiAnn Mills?
   ❏ Very much! I would like to see more books by this author!
   ❏ Moderately. I would have enjoyed it more if

   _____

   _____

   _____

2. Are you a member of **Heartsong Presents**? ❏ Yes ❏ No
   If no, where did you purchase this book? _____

   _____

3. How would you rate, on a scale from 1 (poor) to 5 (superior),
   the cover design? _____

4. On a scale from 1 (poor) to 10 (superior), please rate the
   following elements.

   ____ Heroine   ____ Plot
   ____ Hero   ____ Inspirational theme
   ____ Setting   ____ Secondary characters

5. These characters were special because?_____

_____

_____

6. How has this book inspired your life?_____

_____

_____

7. What settings would you like to see covered in future **Heartsong Presents** books? _____

_____

_____

8. What are some inspirational themes you would like to see treated in future books? _____

_____

_____

9. Would you be interested in reading other **Heartsong Presents** titles? ❏ Yes ❏ No

10. Please check your age range:
   ❏ Under 18   ❏ 18-24
   ❏ 25-34   ❏ 35-45
   ❏ 46-55   ❏ Over 55

Name _____

Occupation _____

Address _____

City_____ State_____ Zip_____

Heartsong

··········· **Presents** ···········

__HP515 *Love Almost Lost*, I. B. Brand
__HP516 *Lucy's Quilt*, J. Livingston
__HP519 *Red River Bride*, C. Coble
__HP520 *The Flame Within*, P. Griffin
__HP523 *Raining Fire*, L. A. Coleman
__HP524 *Laney's Kiss*, T. V. Bateman
__HP531 *Lizzie*, L. Ford
__HP532 *A Promise Made*, J. L. Barton
__HP535 *Viking Honor*, D. Mindrup
__HP536 *Emily's Place*, T. V. Bateman
__HP539 *Two Hearts Wait*, F. Chrisman
__HP540 *Double Exposure*, S. Laity
__HP543 *Cora*, M. Colvin
__HP544 *A Light Among Shadows*, T. H. Murray
__HP547 *Maryelle*, L. Ford
__HP548 *His Brother's Bride*, D. Hunter
__HP551 *Healing Heart*, R. Druten
__HP552 *The Vicar's Daughter*, K. Comeaux
__HP555 *But For Grace*, T. V. Bateman
__HP556 *Red Hills Stranger*, M. G. Chapman
__HP559 *Banjo's New Song*, R. Dow
__HP560 *Heart Appearances*, P. Griffin
__HP563 *Redeemed Hearts*, C. M. Hake
__HP564 *Tender Hearts*, K. Dykes
__HP567 *Summer Dream*, M. H. Flinkman
__HP568 *Loveswept*, T. H. Murray
__HP571 *Bayou Fever*, K. Y'Barbo
__HP572 *Temporary Husband*, D. Mills
__HP575 *Kelly's Chance*, W. E. Brunstetter

__HP576 *Letters from the Enemy*, S. M. Warren
__HP579 *Grace*, L. Ford
__HP580 *Land of Promise*, C. Cox
__HP583 *Ramshakle Rose*, C. M. Hake
__HP584 *His Brother's Castoff*, L. N. Dooley
__HP587 *Lilly's Dream*, P. Darty
__HP588 *Torey's Prayer*, T. V. Bateman
__HP591 *Eliza*, M. Colvin
__HP592 *Refining Fire*, C. Cox
__HP595 *Surrendered Heart*, J. Odell
__HP596 *Kiowa Husband*, D. Mills
__HP599 *Double Deception*, L. Nelson Dooley
__HP600 *The Restoration*, C. M. Hake
__HP603 *A Whale of a Marriage*, D. Hunt
__HP604 *Irene*, L. Ford
__HP607 *Protecting Amy*, S. P. Davis
__HP608 *The Engagement*, K. Comeaux
__HP611 *Faithful Traitor*, J. Stengl
__HP612 *Michaela's Choice*, L. Harris
__HP615 *Gerda's Lawman*, L. N. Dooley
__HP616 *The Lady and the Cad*, T. H. Murray
__HP619 *Everlasting Hope*, T. V. Bateman
__HP620 *Basket of Secrets*, D. Hunt
__HP623 *A Place Called Home*, J. L. Barton
__HP624 *One Chance in a Million*, C. M. Hake
__HP627 *He Loves Me, He Loves Me Not*,
　　　　　R. Druten
__HP628 *Silent Heart*, B. Youree

Great Inspirational Romance at a Great Price!

Heartsong Presents books are inspirational romances in contemporary and historical settings, designed to give you an enjoyable, spirit-lifting reading experience. You can choose wonderfully written titles from some of today's best authors like Peggy Darty, Sally Laity, DiAnn Mills, Colleen L. Reece, Debra White Smith, and many others.

When ordering quantities less than twelve, above titles are $2.97 each.
Not all titles may be available at time of order.